THE UNDERDOG

SAGIT SCHWARTZ

First paperback edition October 2025

Cover image by at Gentle_Veenus
Cover font by Sarah_and_Dipitous

ISBN: 979-8-9921214-0-7

www.sagitschwartz.com

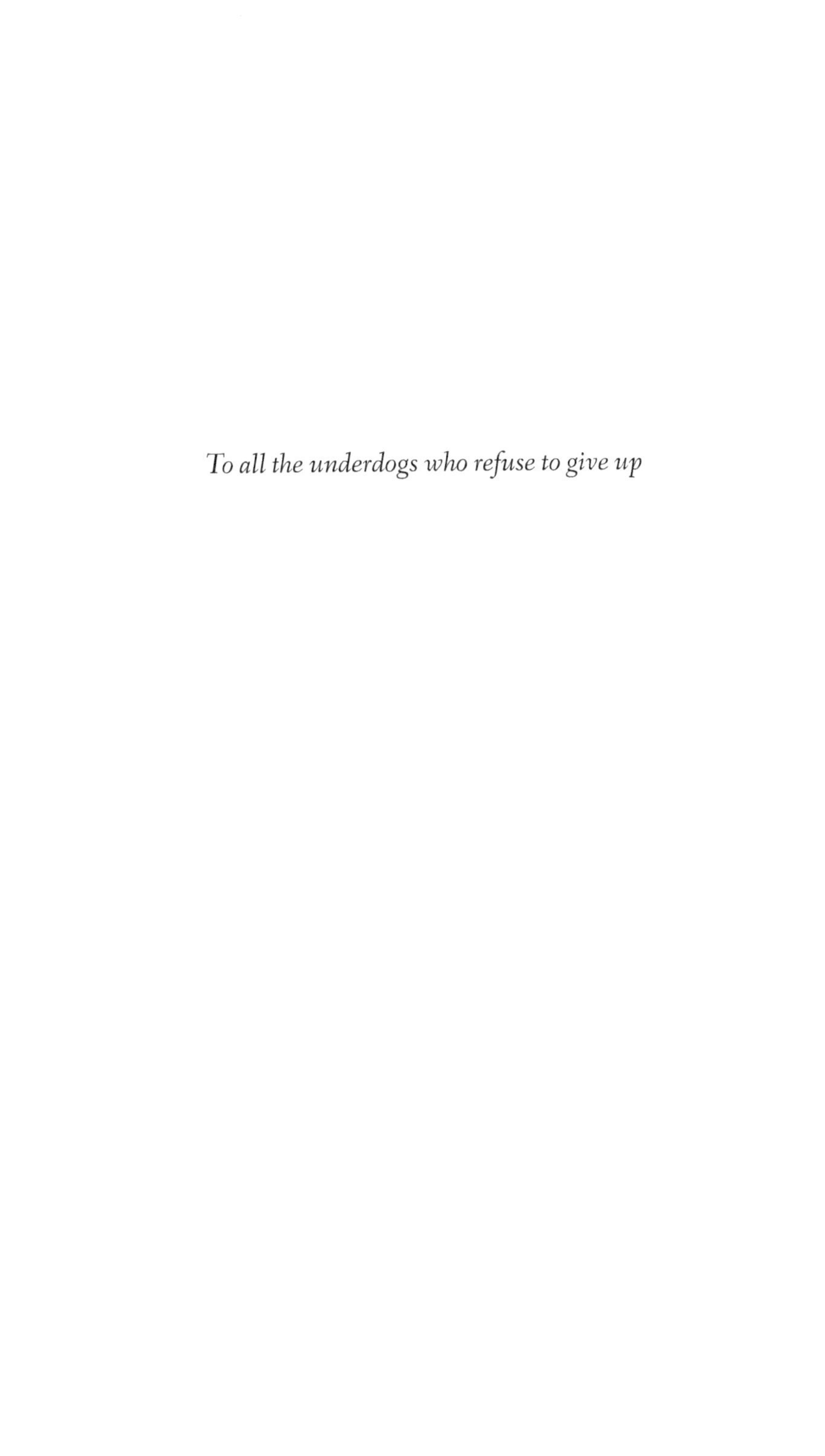

To all the underdogs who refuse to give up

*Everyone loves a comeback story,
and everyone loves the underdog.*
—James Arthur

*Life, which can be strangely merciful, had taken pity on
Norma Desmond. The dream she had clung to so desperately
had enfolded her.*
—Joe Gillis, *Sunset Boulevard*

ONE

LIZ

Day One
Saturday, July 3, 2021

I'm standing in front of Bell Psychiatric Hospital, staring at the glass sliding doors.

My chest fills with dread.

The same unmistakable dread each time an email from Fanny Mae hits my inbox, reminding me of the $235,913.50 debt that will likely follow me to my grave.

Nine years ago, after a stinging divorce, I decided to bet on myself and chase a lifelong dream: apply to the American Film Institute (AFI) to become a director. After I got in, I quit my job as a hospital physical therapist, enrolled, and took out student loans.

Two years later, at the age of twenty-nine, I thought I had it made when I graduated at the top of my AFI class with a short film that I wrote and directed—a Second-Chance Romance with a dash of Magical Realism that was under consideration for an Oscar nomination.

But the nomination never came, and years of low-level

Hollywood jobs followed. A production assistant on a Lifetime Television digital series that never aired. An associate floor director for a daytime talk show, where I held up signs: **APPLAUD**, **QUIET**, **LAUGH**. An assistant location scout where I got trapped at the Scientology headquarters in Hollywood after a day of scouting and wasn't allowed to exit the gates until I messaged the producers an SOS.

When the industry gigs dried up, I took industry-adjacent jobs. A ride operator at Universal Studios. A stint as a sushi server at a Japanese restaurant near the Creative Arts Agency. A dog-walking job for a B-list actor who ended up leaving the business, which left me unemployed again.

But this time, I couldn't find any work because the pandemic hit. I lost my apartment and ended up living in my car until six months ago, when a former AFI professor, Erika, contacted me about a new reality TV music show that her friend was producing.

What sets *The Underdog* apart from its *American Idol* and *The Voice* competitors is that it features contestants from questionable backgrounds. I'm their chaperone, which is why I'm standing in front of Bell Psychiatric Hospital.

I watched a leaked video of the patient, the contestant I'm about to pick up on TikTok. She was singing a stripped-down version of Cher's *Believe* in a mint green hospital gown while the hospital staff stood around her mesmerized.

The comments underneath the TikTok were a river of praise:

Wow. Wow. WOW!!! She made me FEEL this song.
So. Damn. Good. She LIVED these lyrics.
If Joni Mitchell and Cher had a baby...
THE SINGING PATIENT!

In a nod to the New York Times bestselling book, *The Silent Patient* by Alex Michaelides, the last comment had 2,049,271 likes, took off, and Jennifer Addis was dubbed *The Singing Patient*.

Rumor is she had a breakdown after having a baby. That was four months ago, and she hasn't spoken a word since, apart from singing.

I asked our assistant casting director, Abby, why Jennifer's family wasn't accompanying her to the sound stage in Burbank. "Her husband is against her doing the show. He wants nothing to do with it," Abby said. "He thinks it's bad for her. I heard her attorney petitioned the courts on her behalf and won. Since she won't speak, I heard she gave her lawyer written instructions."

"If her husband's worried about her, why wouldn't he want to go with her?" I asked.

Abby shrugged. "Maybe he's busy taking care of their baby."

"How about her parents?" I asked.

"Dead," Abby said.

I looked up the husband, Kevin, online. His LinkedIn profile showed that he graduated with a business degree from Webster University in Saint Louis and is a self-employed accountant.

I wish he were here with me and I weren't alone. The last contestant pick-up scarred me—a blind nine-year-old Ukrainian orphan or an adult female with dwarfism, depending on who you believe. When an American family adopted Svetlana, the Mom claimed she wasn't a girl and, in fact, a grown woman who had tried to kill her—twice. After the alleged second attempt, the family released her back to foster care.

A year ago, she went viral after singing *Spirit Lead*

Me while playing the piano at a Boys and Girls Club that was featured on a *Dateline* episode. One of our producers remembered watching the episode and recruited her for *The Underdog* when the show went into production.

I met Svetlana at LAX. A flight attendant brought her to me as she was a supposed minor flying alone. She was chewing gum, wore sunglasses, and used a walking stick to guide herself.

I helped her into the town car, waiting to take us to the sound stage. Once inside, she pressed the button for the privacy screen to separate us from the driver. I wondered how she knew where it was since she couldn't see.

After the partition was up, she removed her sunglasses, and I saw the crowfeet wrinkles around her eyes. She definitely wasn't a nine-year-old girl, and she wasn't blind, either.

My mouth hung open in shock. Before I could get out a word, she stabbed my big right toe with her pretend walking stick.

"Ow!" I yelped as she placed her pointer finger over my lips.

"I'm from New Jersey," she whispered. "If you expose me, I know people who know people."

My palms clammed up in a nervous sweat. My stomach somersaulted. I didn't say a word to her for the rest of the ride, staring out the window, trying to avoid her gaze.

When we finally got to the studio lot, I tried to get out of the car and realized I was stuck. I yanked myself up and saw a long string of white gum—the liar from New Jersey's gum —connecting my pants to the seat cushion. I looked over at Svetlana, who flashed me a wicked smile. For the rest of the day, whenever I passed her, she poked her pretend walking stick at the white spot on my black pants from the gum spot I had unsuccessfully tried to scrape off.

She's still on the show. I haven't told anyone the truth about her, because I need this job. I never, *ever* want to go back to living in my car.

My phone makes a sound. A text from my pick-up contact at the hospital: **She's ready for you.**

I swallow hard and step inside.

TWO

NORMA

Thirteen Months Earlier
June 2020

When Norma opened the Papyrus card, she knew who it was from.

She had given her daughter, Cookie, the stationary for her birthday, hoping it might inspire her only child to write her a card once in a while.

One of the most painful realizations of motherhood was knowing Cookie would never be able to adequately thank Norma for the countless sacrifices she had made for her.

As Norma read the card, she could barely make sense of the words in front of her:

This letter is to inform you I'm going no-contact. Don't try to reach out. If you come by my house, I'll file a restraining order. Being pregnant has been clarifying. With the help of my therapist, I realize I need to protect my—

Norma stopped reading and closed the card. She stared at the beautiful pile of pastel macaroons on its cover. She bought these cards for Cookie because they reminded her of their first high tea together on Cookie's fifth birthday. Along with the cucumber cream cheese sandwiches, they had served macaroons. Norma remembered how Cookie couldn't pronounce the word "macaroon" and kept calling them "moon."

A sudden sob escaped Norma, thinking back on this sweet memory filled with so much hope and possibility of what lay ahead for them as mother and daughter in contrast to the ugly letter she had just received.

Why was Cookie doing this?

Norma had only ever tried to be helpful to her daughter, especially after Cookie had told her she was pregnant. Norma had offered to pick up items for her future grandchild, but Cookie and her fiancé, Liam, insisted they wanted to do all the baby preparation alone.

Norma had also proposed accompanying Cookie to her doctor's appointments when Liam was too busy with work to be there. But they told her it was unnecessary.

Maybe it was by design. Perhaps a plan to shut her out had long been in motion.

But why?

And why had Cookie chosen *this card* to let Norma know she was going no-contact?

Was it on purpose—to hurt her *even more?*

Maybe Cookie didn't remember Norma had gifted her the cards. She probably didn't remember their first high tea together either.

Norma decided to give *Dateline* a try. Even though it scared her sometimes, like the episode about the ice pick serial killer, at least it was interesting. This episode was about a poor Ukrainian orphan whose adoptive American parents abandoned her because they claimed she was really an adult woman with dwarfism.

Back in the day, when it was in vogue, Norma had briefly considered leaving her family. She had watched several of her contemporaries give up their housewife lives to pursue their dreams. But Norma stuck it out, sacrificing a medical career she had always dreamt of for her late husband and daughter.

Now look where it had gotten her: estrangement.

Norma watched the Ukrainian orphan sing *Spirit Lead Me* while playing the piano at a Boys and Girls Club. It was a stirring performance that brought Norma to tears again. The orphan didn't look like an adult. She looked like a child —an abandoned one.

Sadly, Norma now knew what it felt like to be abandoned.

After *Dateline* was over, she opened the TikTok app on her cell phone. She had downloaded it after the *Dancing With The Stars* host suggested that viewers follow the show on TikTok. She had created her Grandma79* username when she found out she was going to become a grandmother after Cookie had told her that her due date was July 9th.

Norma typed **Dateline** in the TikTok search bar. The orphan's rendition of *Spirit Lead Me* immediately popped up. She watched the magical performance again and read the comments underneath.

ANOINTED for GOD'S GLORY!
CHILLS. A gift straight from heaven.
How could anyone abandon this sweet angel?

Norma had never posted anything on social media

before and debated adding a comment. But her emotions overtook her, and she went for it:

Grandma79*:
Has anyone been abandoned by their daughter?

WHEN NORMA OPENED HER EYES, she looked out the window and saw it was dark out. She had fallen asleep on the couch, watching television, too upset to move her body to her bedroom.

She lifted her cell phone to see what time it was and noticed a notification from the TikTok app—a response to her question.

Janie021351:
Join our Mothers of Estranged Daughters Facebook group. DM me.

THREE
LIZ

Day One
Saturday, July 3, 2021

I anxiously wait at the nurse's station for Jennifer Addis. She's by far the most famous contestant *The Underdog* has landed.

Ever since she went viral singing Cher's *Believe*, the public has been obsessed with trying to figure out why she won't speak and only sings. Some speculate she's sending messages through her song choices. Others think she's gone mad to the point of no return. But everyone is waiting for the day she finally speaks to explain herself, and *The Underdog* producers are hoping it'll happen *on air*.

Doug, my messianic complex-riddled boss, who's only good at two things—barking orders or threatening me, warned me before I left: "We're expecting Super Bowl ratings. Do *not* fuck this up, or you'll be out of a job."

He knows how desperate I am. The day I interviewed, he found me sleeping in my car in the studio parking lot. I had arrived early and accidentally passed out. When I lived out of my car, I made sure to park in good neighborhoods at night. Still, I never slept well. Always on edge that something bad might happen in the middle of the night with no one to save me. Whenever I got to a safe space like the gated studio parking lot, my body had the habit of collapsing.

Doug found me asleep and knocked on my window. I jumped up, startled, and saw him staring at me through the glass. He also peered behind me into the backseat of my car. Some of my belongings that I couldn't fit in the trunk of my car were peeking out from underneath the silver windshield sunshade.

Twenty minutes later, when I showed up for my interview and discovered he was the one interviewing me, I almost turned around and left. I thought I had no chance of being hired. I assumed he had figured out that I was living out of my car. But I didn't want to make Erika look bad, who had helped get me the interview and sucked it up and went through with it.

When I stepped inside Doug's office, the movie *Amadeus* was playing on a television screen mounted on the wall behind his desk. He spent the entire interview bitterly complaining that, like Mozart, he was a misunderstood genius and that Hollywood was his Salieri, forever jealous of his talents due to their mediocrity. He explained that was the reason why he worked at *The Underdog* instead of being an Oscar-winning film producer.

After the interview ended, I assumed I wouldn't get the job due to our parking lot exchange. But to my surprise, the very next day, I got an offer. It turns out it's easier to have an underling who's too desperate to ever go to HR to file a complaint against you.

A loud thump jolts me. "This is her suitcase," a hospital security guard with thick brows says, pointing to a silver aluminum suitcase. "I went through it. Everything inside is safe."

Safe?

He steps aside as Jennifer Addis and a nurse exit a room together and approach me.

Jennifer is petite and is wearing black sweatpants and white custom-made canvas low-top shoes with black musical notes painted on them. I wonder if someone had them made for her to wear on the show. Her brown hair is pulled back in a ponytail, and she has lavender AirPods in her ears. I've never seen colored AirPods before. Maybe those were custom-made for her too.

"Hi, I'm Betsy," the nurse says. She looks like a silver sister, or at least pictures I've seen of them online—tall, striking, with a long mane of silver hair. "This is our singing patient—Jennifer."

"I like your shoes," I tell Jennifer, trying to break the ice.

A blonde, muscular woman with large pearl earrings and a stethoscope around her neck walks up to us.

"Hello, I'm Dr. Clara Griffin," she tells me. "These are Jennifer's medications. Instructions are inside the bag. If you have any questions, please don't hesitate to contact me." Dr. Griffin hands me a ziplock bag with a couple of prescription bottles.

I'm in charge of her medicine?

"Okay," I say and take the bag from her.

"We'll see you both back in a few days," Dr. Griffin says.

"Unless she makes it to the next round!" Betsy chimes in, smiling.

"Everyone here is excited," Dr. Griffin says. She turns to Jennifer and smiles. "We're proud of you."

I look at Jennifer, who's the only one not smiling.

A DRIVER TAKES us to the airport. Every once in a while, I look up from my phone and watch Jennifer staring out the window with the lavender AirPods in her ears.

"You're a great singer," I say, unsure if she can hear me.

She briefly turns around to face me.

"I'm an artist too. A filmmaker. I graduated from AFI," I nervously say, trying to align with her.

She doesn't say a word and turns back around to face the window.

WE CHECK in and walk toward our gate when Jennifer stops in front of a restroom. She silently stares at me like she's waiting for me to say something.

"Do you need to use it?" I ask her.

She nods her head.

"Okay, let's go," I say. She walks inside, and I'm about to follow her when my cell phone makes a sound.

A text from Doug: **Update ASAP.**

She's using the restroom. Headed to the gate after, I text back.

You with her??? he texts.

Of course, I text back.

I slip my phone into my bag, step inside the bathroom, and scan the bottom of the stalls for her white canvas low tops with black keynotes. I spot them in the second to last stall and walk up to her.

"Jennifer, I'm here," I say, even though I don't expect a response. "I'll wait for you by the sinks."

I walk over to a row of sinks and position myself in a

small space between a soap dispenser and a hand air dryer on the adjacent wall.

I take out my phone again and scroll through a stream of emails. One from the line producer about the contestants I need to pick up for the wildcard contestant round in a few days. Another from casting checking in on today's pick-up. And, on cue, an email from Fannie Mae reminding me they own me.

"Excuse us," a mom with a toddler son says. I look up and see she's standing with her boy, whose hands are dripping with water. I move to the side so they can access the dryer, which gusts forceful cold air that blows on the side of my left arm.

I return my phone to my bag and turn my attention back to Jennifer's stall. I don't see her shoes. She's probably using the toilet now, and her feet don't touch the ground because she's petite.

I walk toward the stall just to make sure. "Jennifer," I say.

She doesn't respond.

"I don't see your feet. Can you sing something to let me know you're there?" I ask.

Still, nothing.

I knock on the door.

"One minute," she says.

I finally got her to speak!

The toilet flushes. The door swings open, but Jennifer Addis isn't standing before me. It's a woman with straight long blonde hair dressed in all black who gives me side-eye as she brushes past me.

Did Jennifer switch stalls? I quickly scan the bottom of each one, but I don't see her shoes.

"Jennifer?" I call out.

She doesn't respond, but why would she? She doesn't speak.

Maybe she's outside waiting for me. I rush out of the bathroom and look around at the Hudson bookstore, a Starbucks, a bar and grill restaurant. Various announcements thunder over the airport bathroom speakers: pre-boarding reminders, plane delays.

But I don't see her anywhere.

Maybe her stall was dirty, or the toilet didn't work, and she switched. I noticed there was a second room with stalls inside the bathroom.

I run back inside to the second room filled with stalls. An airport employee with a badge steering an older woman in a wheelchair almost rolls over my foot. I scan the bottom of each stall, searching for Jennifer's low tops, which I don't see. I then physically move from stall to stall, looking underneath to see if her feet are hanging and not touching the ground due to her being petite.

"Jennifer?" I say at least a half dozen times.

Relief washes over me when I spot her lavender AirPod on the ground in front of the very last stall—the one hugging the bathroom wall near the exit.

"You dropped your AirPod," I say.

She doesn't say anything. My mouth goes dry when I notice the door is slightly ajar. I crack it open.

Nobody's inside.

Jennifer Addis is gone.

FOUR

NORMA

Thirteen Months Earlier
June 2020

Norma sat at Starbucks nervously, clutching her paper coffee cup. She wore her favorite white prairie dress with embroidered front patch pockets. She had put on a thick coat of coral lipstick and checked her teeth to ensure no lipstick was on them because she wanted to make a good impression on her new friend.

Norma and Janie from TikTok and the Mothers of Estranged Daughters Facebook group Norma had joined had become fast friends over the last week, messaging and communicating multiple times a day.

After Norma received Janie's message to DM her, she Googled "DM" and discovered it meant "direct message." She then watched a YouTube tutorial video about how to message on TikTok and sent one to Janie asking if she'd be welcomed into the Facebook group.

Norma couldn't bear being rejected again after

receiving Cookie's letter. Janie let her know that there were over four thousand members and reassured her that she'd be more than welcome. But Norma still wasn't sure, so she asked Janie what her zodiac sign was. When Janie told her she was a Sagittarius, Norma knew she could trust her.

"I like Sagittarians," Norma messaged her.

After Norma joined the group, Janie and her friended each other on Facebook and started messaging there. Shortly after, they switched to communicating via FaceTime.

In the evenings, when Norma's heart ached the most, thinking about what Cookie had done, she reached out to Janie, who was there to support her. Janie shared that her daughter, Luanne, had abandoned her as soon as she turned eighteen. At first, Janie thought it was due to drug addiction. But to her surprise, Luanne went to college, then graduate school to get her MBA, and now worked in finance as an analyst for McKinsey, which Janie only knew about because of Luanne's LinkedIn profile.

Janie had tried reaching out to Luanne through the years to no avail, including mailing her birthday presents each year until the Meta algorithm pushed out an Instagram reel to Janie, showing Luanne opening her estranged mother's yearly birthday gifts for the world to see.

That's when Janie knew she needed support from others in her shoes. It was one thing to deal with the pain of losing her daughter alone, but watching her daughter make a mockery of her in the public square was more heartache than she could withstand alone.

It turned out that Janie and Norma lived only an hour's drive from each other. Norma was happy to drive to meet her new friend in person. She arrived early at Starbucks and texted Janie, asking what she should order for her—a hot cappuccino—that was now waiting for her.

Norma took a sip of coffee when she saw her new friend entering the coffee shop. Janie looked effortlessly chic, dressed in camel pants and a white blouse. Her hair was pulled back in a tight bun. She wore large diamond studs. A matching tennis bracelet hung from her wrist.

Norma felt self-conscious, almost provincial, in her vintage prairie dress, even though she had purchased it at Anthropologie, and it had cost a lot. She smiled and waved to Janie, who waved back.

When Janie approached her and hugged Norma, Norma didn't want to let go. She had felt unbearably alone since receiving Cookie's card.

"Thank you for meeting me," Norma said.

"This is a treat," Janie said, sitting down. "I've only met two other group members in person."

"This may seem silly, but I'm still hoping to turn things around," Norma admitted.

"I understand," Janie said. "It took me three years to accept my new reality, but I promise you that there's life on the other side."

"I just don't understand why Cookie is doing this," Norma said.

"Therapy is to blame," Janie explained. "It's marketing itself to millennials. Not because it's healing. It's a for-profit business. Bad actors are looking to profit off of made-up reasons for parental estrangement. With no basis, they diagnose us with a cluster of personality disorders. It's this generation's version of repressed memories. Our daughters are being used."

That rang a bell for Norma because she had overheard Cookie talking to Liam about a therapy appointment. And

Cookie also mentioned a therapist in her no-contact letter to Norma.

If only there was a way for Norma to have a heart-to-heart talk with Cookie to try and make her understand she was being used and brainwashed. But it wasn't possible without risking Cookie filing a restraining order against her. The best Norma could hope for was to find a way to still be in her future grandchild's life.

"I don't think it's fair that I'll be deprived of seeing my grandchild," Norma said. "Do you know if grandparents have rights?"

"A child's parents have the right to decide whether or not their child will see their grandparent or anyone for that matter," Janie said.

Norma's eyes bubbled with tears. She looked down because she didn't want her new friend, who seemed to have it all together, to see her pain.

"But if the parents don't live together, either parent can let the child see whoever they want during their parenting time," Janie continued.

A glimmer of hope.

Norma looked up. "So you mean if Cookie's fiancé and her don't live together, either one has the individual right to allow me to see my grandchild?"

"Yes, unless there's some court order stopping you. This comes up in the group a lot," Janie said.

Norma nodded her head, taking in the information. The problem was that Cookie was smitten with Liam, and they weren't headed for a breakup anytime soon, especially now with a baby on the way.

Norma worried that Cookie was only with him because he was the first man who had paid any attention to her, except for Cookie's brief high school boyfriend. Because of this, it seemed Liam always got his way in their relationship, from big decisions like where they would live to minor ones like choosing which restaurants they frequented.

Norma had only seen them have one argument where Cookie got her way. It was about the hospital where she wanted to deliver. Liam was against it because he had been to their emergency room and had a bad experience. But Cookie was adamant about giving birth there because her doctor was affiliated with the hospital. "I'm the one giving birth. I get to decide," she had told Liam, who let it go.

But even if Cookie weren't smitten with Liam, Norma would never want to put a wedge between her daughter and her fiancé. Norma had never put her own interests before her daughter. She had sacrificed her entire life for her.

But then, Norma realized something. Maybe she needed to do this for Cookie, because Cookie was being brainwashed, and Liam wasn't aware. Nobody would save Cookie unless Norma intervened.

If she could somehow create a temporary rift between Liam and Cookie, she might be able to get Liam on her side, who would be far more able to convince Cookie that a therapist had used her.

Even better, if Cookie found herself alone and pregnant, maybe it would be enough to snap her out of her trance. She would realize the value of having a grandmother around to help with a baby and be inclined to reach out to Norma.

Once Cookie was deprogrammed, Norma could explain to her daughter what she had done and why she had done it. Cookie would understand because Norma had saved her.

Creating a fracture in Cookie and Liam's relationship was actually in Cookie's best interest. And Norma's entire life had been dedicated to her daughter.

Norma looked up at her new friend. "Thank you for letting me know."

"Here to help," Janie said and kept talking.

But Norma's mind was elsewhere. She knew what she had to do.

The problem was she had no idea how.

FIVE

LIZ

Day One
Saturday, July 3, 2021

"You waited for her inside the restroom?" A female TSA agent with the name tag Gonzalez pinned to her uniform shirt asks me.

After Jennifer disappeared, I went to our gate, spoke to a United employee at the counter, and explained the situation. He called for Jennifer multiple times on the loudspeaker, telling her where to meet me.

After forty-five minutes, she never showed up, and he contacted airport personnel. Gonzalez met me there and had me follow her to an elevator down three floors, where she ushered me into a private room with fluorescent lights. I'm sitting across from her on a beige fold-up chair with a metal desk between us.

"Yes," I say. "I waited for her inside the bathroom by the sinks."

"And you didn't notice her leaving?" Gonzalez says.

"There was a lot of commotion with travelers going in

and out, and I was checking work emails on my phone," I say and immediately regret it.

"So you were busy on your phone and gave her the chance to take off?" Gonzalez asks.

It feels more like an accusation than a question, but I know better than to push back. I've read enough terrifying accounts on Reddit about TSA agents drunk with power who can put you on a no-fly list if you sneeze the wrong way. And I need to get back to LA.

"I looked away for a couple of minutes at most," I say. "I found one of her AirPods near a stall by an exit. She must've run out quickly."

I take out the purple AirPod from my bag and place it on the metal desk between us.

Gonzalez glances at it. "You said you picked her up from a psych hospital?"

"Yes," I say.

"Sounds like she's not someone you should've taken your eyes off of for a second," Gonzalez says.

My phone won't stop making sounds. I'm sure it's Doug letting me know I'm fired since I've gone dark for the last hour.

"I think my boss may be trying to reach me," I say.

Gonzalez ignores my comment. "Why isn't her family with you?"

"Our casting director told me her husband didn't want her doing the show," I say.

The door swings open.

A police officer in his mid-thirties with jet-black hair and a no-nonsense gait steps inside, carrying a laptop. "Detective Cooper," he announces, taking a seat next to Gonzalez across from me. "We understand you were responsible for Jennifer Addis when she disappeared?"

His using her full name makes me feel like I'm in even more trouble.

"Yes," I say. "I'm the contestant chaperone for *The Underdog*."

"Where exactly were you waiting for Ms. Addis?" he asks.

"Inside the bathroom near her stall," I answer.

"You sure about that?" He says.

"Yes," I say.

"Our team is reviewing footage from every airport camera in the United terminal now..."

He lets that sentence hang in the air like it will change my story.

"Hopefully, you'll be able to see where she went," I say.

"Are you aware that Ms. Addis is the sole heir of a large family fortune?" Cooper says.

"No," I say.

"Her father owned one of the largest warehouse companies in the Midwest, which she recently inherited after he died," he continues.

"I don't know anything about her except that she was hospitalized after she had a baby and that she sings well," I say.

Cooper nods his head, unconvinced. "We've done a background check on you...lots of debt," he says.

Why's he bringing that up?

"I got my Master's degree from the American Film Institute. It was very expensive," I say, even though I don't owe him an explanation.

"And you're working at *The Underdog* now?" he asks.

I sit up straighter. "I had a short film that was almost nominated for an Oscar," I say.

"When?" he says.

"A while ago," I say, not wanting to admit it was nine years ago.

Right after I graduated from AFI, whenever I'd run into former classmates, they'd ask me what I was working on. I'd mention the producers and A-list actresses reading the feature adaptation I'd written of my short, which they all knew was under consideration for an Oscar. But as the years passed and nothing came of it or my career, if I ran into them, I'd try to hide to avoid seeing them due to my shame.

Sometimes, I couldn't duck in time; they'd approach me and ask what I was doing. I'd deflect awkwardly. Eventually, it didn't matter because they stopped asking altogether, which was even worse. A reminder that a life once filled with such promise had all but disappeared.

"A buddy of mine graduated from AFI," Cooper says, pulling me out of memories. "He makes movies for Sony now."

Cooper sure knows how to twist the knife. I know I'm not the young, bright, shiny object that I once was after I graduated from AFI. And some may call it delusional, but I still dream of making great films like *Sunset Boulevard*, *Michael Clayton*, and *You've Got Mail*. I still hold out the hope that one day I'll follow the careers of other great female directors like Kathryn Bigelow, Ava DuVernay, and my romcom hero, Nora Ephron.

"Everyone's path is different," I tell Cooper.

"You must not make a lot at *The Underdog* with your kind of debt," Cooper says.

"It's enough to keep a roof over my head," I say.

"People like Jennifer Addis are in a position to pay people like you to look the other way…"

Wait a second, *does he think Jennifer Addis paid me off?*

"Do you have anything you want to tell us about your $235,913.50 Fanny Mae loan?" he asks, opening the laptop he carried into the room.

"I'm worried I'll die with it," I admit. "But I hope that one day I'll have the career I've always dreamt of and be able to pay it off."

"Looks like your dreams are about to come true," he says, turning the laptop screen to face me.

My name, contact information, and student loan number are pulled up on the screen with three words I've dreamt of reading for the last nine years: **PAID IN FULL**.

SIX

NORMA

Thirteen Months Earlier
June 2020

The idea had come to Norma in the middle of the night. She knew Liam had a wandering eye. On several occasions, she had seen him gaze a little too long at young waitresses when she had gone out for dinner with him and Cookie.

Norma placed a for-hire ad in her local town's community paper, looking for an actress to pretend her car broke down near Liam and Cookie's house. Cookie didn't work from home, but Liam did. When the actress rang their doorbell, Liam would be the one to answer.

The other part of Norma's plan involved hiring a private detective to take pictures of Liam and the young actress together. If Liam looked at the young woman like Norma had seen him look at waitresses, this would be a slam dunk.

Norma met the only actress who responded to her ad at a local diner near her home and explained the job. Ruby was young, beautiful, and had Julia Roberts long auburn hair.

"My daughter's fiancé is a bad man," Norma explained. "I caught him cheating on her and told her, but she didn't believe me. Now that she's pregnant, I need to show her proof. That's where you come in. I need you to show up at their house. A P.I. will take pictures of you two together."

This wasn't exactly what Ruby had in mind when she studied acting in college.

"This is really dark," Ruby said.

"I'll pay you five hundred dollars for a ten-minute job," Norma said. "You know as well as I do that my daughter should get out before the baby arrives."

Ruby nodded. She didn't disagree, and it was hard to pass up five hundred dollars.

"I don't want my face in those pictures," Ruby said.

"I'll make sure the P.I. blurs it out," Norma told her.

THE PLAN HAD GONE PERFECTLY. The P.I. sent Norma copies of the pictures with Ruby's face blurred out. In one photo, it looked like Liam was smiling at Ruby adoringly. In another, he put his hand on her arm while ushering her to her car. There was no way Cookie would stick with Liam after she saw these pictures.

Norma was parked down the block from their house. She had slid down in her car seat, barely peeking above the driver's side window. Nobody, including Cookie, could see her.

The P.I. had just dropped off the manila envelope with the pictures on the welcome mat. He rang the doorbell before quickly disappearing.

Norma watched as Cookie opened the front door and picked up the envelope. She looked inside and removed the pictures.

Norma waited with bated breath for her daughter to fall apart. Tears. Sobs. Maybe even screams. But Cookie shuffled through the pictures nonplussed—and *rolled her eyes*.

SEVEN

LIZ

Day One
Saturday, July 3, 2021

I stare at Cooper's laptop screen.

"That's a mistake," I say. "I just got an email reminder today about my upcoming monthly payment."

"The email you received was sent early this morning. Your loan was paid off after Jennifer Addis disappeared."

"Nobody knows about my loan. I've never told anyone about it—not even my Dad."

"We'll make sure to follow up with him," Cooper says.

I swallow hard, thinking about Dad getting a call from the police. He raised me on his own after Mom died when I was twelve. He supported me when I gave up my physical therapy hospital job to chase my directing dream. *"You only live once, Lizzie,"* he told me.

I never told him about my student loans or living out of my car. I only briefly considered it when I started living out of my car and unsuccessfully tried getting my old hospital job back. It had been years, and my former boss told me there were no open positions. She also reminded me that my continuing education units weren't up to date.

I had no money to take classes and thought about asking Dad if I could move in with him in the suburban house outside of Chicago where I grew up until I got back on my feet. But I couldn't bear to do it. I couldn't break his heart again. He already had it broken once when Mom died.

I've always wanted him to believe I was successful. He deserves to feel a sense of pride that he did a good job of raising me on his own because he did.

"In the meantime, our accounting forensics team will be busy tracking down how this loan was paid off and *who* paid it," Cooper continues.

"Are you sure it was paid off?" I ask.

"Yes. You didn't read this?" he says, pointing to the computer screen.

"What?" I say.

Cooper points to two small lines underneath **PAID IN FULL**, which I hadn't noticed.

We're pleased to let you know we've received the funds to pay off this loan. If the funds we received were too much, we'll send you a check for the extra amount.

"If whoever paid off your loan overpaid it," he says. "You'll be getting a nice check in the mail—one that may allow you never to have to work again for the rest of your life."

"But I want to work," I insist. "I want to be a filmmaker."

"You're not doing that now," Cooper says sharply. "But

a nice payoff from Jennifer Addis would help. The problem for you is that she's a fugitive. And under 18 US Code section 752, there's a penalty of up to five years imprisonment and fines for a person who instigates, aids, or assists a person's escape or attempts to escape."

EIGHT

NORMA

One Year Earlier
July 2020

Norma showed up at the hospital for her volunteer training session, her lips painted in her signature coral lipstick and wearing her prairie dress. She hoped being there would take her mind off things.

A couple of weeks had passed, and she had gotten in an obsessive loop over her failed attempt to put a wedge between Liam and Cookie. For the life of her, she couldn't figure out why Cookie had rolled her eyes at the compromising pictures of Liam and Ruby together.

Maybe there was more to Liam's wandering eye. Maybe he was a serial cheater. Maybe Cookie was used to this and had grown to accept it.

Norma had driven by their house several times and saw they were still very much a couple. She watched Liam help a pregnant Cookie into her car. She saw them walking arm and arm together, laughing after a night out.

Norma hadn't told Janie and her Facebook support

group about what she had done. Not because it was wrong —it wasn't. She had tried to save her daughter.

She didn't mention it because she was new to the group and didn't know if they'd understand since they seemed to advocate a more hands-off approach to dealing with estranged adult children.

Instead, Norma posted about the pain and grief she was feeling due to losing Cookie. Several members encouraged her to find meaning in her life apart from her daughter through God or volunteering.

When she stepped inside the hospital nursery to meet the volunteer coordinator, she looked at the rows of newborn babies and felt a swell of sadness bloom inside of her. She thought about how she would never be able to meet her future grandchild. Maybe volunteering hadn't been a good idea.

Seeing the newborns also reminded Norma of how she had felt when she held Cookie for the first time after Cookie was born. The constant agita she experienced due to her bottled-up dreams finally quieted down, even if becoming a mother hadn't been her first choice.

There had been a time when Norma had big dreams. Far too big for a woman of her generation. She might have been able to become a teacher, a nurse, or maybe a social worker, but Norma had wanted to become a doctor.

She had been smart enough. Always at the top of her class, beating out all the boys and getting pushback for it. Not just from the other students but also from teachers, who were eager to keep her in a little box. Back then, intelligent girls weren't rewarded. They were ostracized.

When Norma became pregnant in college, it made it easier for her to stop wrestling with something society would never let her be. She would become a mother, and after holding Cookie for the first time, she was grateful to have found something that quelled the pain and longing of her unrealized dreams. Norma's life finally had meaning.

But the problems started almost immediately after Cookie was born. Because Cookie didn't stay a baby. With each passing day, week, and month, she grew. And with each passing year, Cookie needed Norma less and less. And the bad feelings returned for Norma.

The worst part was Norma had a front-row seat to watching her daughter chase her dreams, something the world had never given Norma the chance to do. If only Cookie knew how painful it had been for Norma to spend her entire life sitting on the sidelines. Forced to watch Cookie get to do whatever she wanted while stuffing down any chance of becoming who she had been destined to be just to be her mother.

And now, what did Norma have to show for putting her daughter first?

No-contact.

Nobody will break your heart like your own child, Norma thought.

A male nurse with sky-blue eyes approached Norma, arousing her from her thoughts.

"Are you here for the training?" he asked.

"Yes," Norma said.

"I'm Jay," he said, smiling with California white teeth. "Come with me."

Norma followed him into a small room where they sat on maroon-colored cushioned chairs. He spoke to her about the necessary qualities to be a successful volunteer—good communication, problem-solving, and teamwork. He explained that she would be making a vital contribution to the hospital by holding babies when their parents couldn't be with them.

After, he taught her how to do CPR on babies using a plastic doll. Norma was an easy study. After all, she had wanted to become a doctor. This was in her wheelhouse, and Jay praised her for her aptitude and focus.

By the end of the first training session, Norma felt good about herself. Valued. For once in her life, she was being treated with the respect she had always deserved.

The support group members were right. Finding meaning in her life apart from Cookie was a good thing.

But Norma also felt sad. If a perfect stranger like Jay could treat her this way, why couldn't her own daughter?

Yes, Cookie had been brainwashed by a therapist, but wasn't she smarter than to fall for a con?

"We'll see you back tomorrow?" Jay asked Norma.

"Yes," she said.

"Thanks again," he said.

Norma left the nursery and headed toward the ladies' room before her drive home. When she turned the corner, she froze.

Liam was there, following a hospital employee with a badge. He smiled wide as they both slipped inside a patient room.

What's he doing here? Norma wondered.

This wasn't the hospital where Cookie was supposed to deliver. Unlike whatever ideas Cookie had about Norma, Norma respected Cookie's boundaries and made sure not to volunteer at the hospital where Cookie had insisted on having her baby.

Yes, Norma had called that hospital in the early stages of researching volunteer opportunities when she was gathering information. It turned out they weren't taking on any new volunteers, but Norma wouldn't have volunteered there anyway, even if they had openings.

Had Cookie changed her mind and decided to deliver at Little Saint Mary's? Were Liam, Cookie, and her newborn grandchild inside the room Liam had just slipped into? Was the hospital employee part of Cookie's delivery team?

Norma stood in place, unsure of what to do next, when Jay snuck up behind her.

"The exit is the other way," Jay told her.

"I need to use the ladies' room before I leave," Norma said.

"It's over there," he said, pointing.

"Thanks," she said.

Norma walked toward the restroom. She wanted to go inside the hospital room where Liam was. But if Cookie was there, they might make a big scene, possibly contact the police, file a restraining order, or ask the hospital security guards to usher her out.

Norma decided to go home and write Cookie a letter instead, which she hoped Liam would give her. Norma would explain the situation, how she was volunteering at Little Saint Mary's because Cookie had insisted on delivering at a different hospital. She would let Cookie know she had seen Liam there and didn't want any issues if either of them saw her while she was volunteering.

Norma hoped against hope that maybe after giving birth, Cookie would be so overcome with emotion that she'd welcome her mother back into the fold.

NORMA DROVE up to Cookie's house with the letter. She considered buying a baby gift, too, but members of the

Facebook support group she had consulted with advised her not to.

Janie reminded Norma that her daughter, Luanne, had shamed her on the internet by opening up her gifts for the world to see. Norma didn't want to risk public humiliation and stuck with the letter.

She exited her car and walked toward Cookie's house with the envelope when she saw a *very pregnant* Cookie in front, carrying two full bags of groceries, one in each arm.

Norma quickly hid behind a tree. She watched Cookie put down the bags, who grabbed her stomach, wincing, before opening the front door and letting herself inside.

Cookie hadn't given birth yet.

So why was Liam at the hospital?

NORMA RETURNED HOME with the letter. It was no good now that she knew Cookie hadn't delivered yet. Norma decided to write something else and email Cookie instead.

Dear Cookie,

I want to let you know that I'm volunteering at Little Saint Mary's because you said you weren't going to deliver there. Today, I saw Liam there. I don't want any problems if I run into either of you. I've respected your boundaries and don't want you to think otherwise.

Love,
Mom

Norma hit send. She wondered if Cookie might file a restraining order against her for the email when Norma's computer made a sound. Cookie had already responded with an email of her own:

Liam was touring the maternity ward because I'm on bed rest. Stay away from both of us. Do <u>NOT</u> email me again.

Norma was confused. Cookie had been carrying grocery bags inside her house. A woman on bed rest wasn't supposed to get up except maybe to use the bathroom. She certainly wasn't supposed to go to the supermarket or carry heavy items.

Why was Cookie lying—and was Liam really on a hospital tour?

NINE

LIZ

Day One
Saturday, July 3, 2021

I arrived at LAX and am now in the town car that was supposed to take Jennifer Addis and me to the sound stage at The Grove shopping center for a practice run before tomorrow night's show. Instead, Doug asked me to go to the studio lot and meet him at his office. I'm sure he wants to fire me in person instead of sparing me the humiliation and letting me go by text or email.

After Detective Cooper let me leave the airport interrogation room at JFK, I ran back to the gate and caught a different flight home since the one Jennifer and I were supposed to catch had already left. Cooper said he'd be following up with me as the police investigate who paid off my loans since he thinks it's connected to Jennifer Addis's disappearance.

I take out my phone, search for the Fanny Mae email I got this morning, and call them.

After pressing multiple numbers and trying to connect

with a human being, I wait for seventeen minutes before a person finally gets on the line. She introduces herself as Sheree.

"My student loan was paid off, and I need to find out who paid it," I explain.

"Wasn't you?" Sheree asks.

"No," I say.

"Lemme see..." she says. "Looks like it was paid off anonymously. Never seen that before."

"I never authorized anyone to pay it off," I say.

"Guess you got lucky," she says. "*Real* lucky."

Some luck.

"I don't want it paid off—" I say before the connection gets fuzzy. I can't hear her for a minute. But then, she returns.

"If you don't mind answering a survey after we hang up about how I handled your question today—" she says before the line goes dead.

The acid in my stomach burns. It's making its way up my throat, tingling.

I'm about to be fired.

Soon, I'll be out of money and back to living in my car unless I come clean to Dad, assuming the police haven't already called him and told him everything. He's going to find out about my student loans and my entanglement in Jennifer Addis's disappearance.

According to Cooper, if the police can connect me to it, I'm staring down five years of imprisonment, not to mention a likely televised trial involving the infamous Singing Patient.

The town car pulls into the studio lot. I thank the driver and get out. I decide not to go to Doug's office so he can fire me in person. I have far bigger worries now, like finding a pro-bono attorney to help me. I head to my office to pack up my things. Hopefully, I can slip out before Doug sees me.

When I open my office door, he's waiting inside for me. "How are you?" he asks.

"I just want to get my stuff and leave," I say.

"Where ya goin?" he says, smiling. I think he's getting off on this.

"To find a lawyer," I say.

"Sounds stressful," he says, in a borderline understanding tone, which confuses me.

"It is stressful when the police falsely accuse you of helping a fugitive escape,"

"Juicy," he says.

I can't with his shit today.

"Thanks for the opportunity," I say. I start picking up things from my desk.

"What are you doing?" he asks.

"Vacating my office. I'm fired," I say.

"Who said anything about firing?" he says.

"I lost the most important contestant of the show. Super Bowl ratings—remember?"

"There's a nationwide hunt for The Singing Patient now," he says. "Rumors are swirling that you're involved. Every news outlet will be covering your every move. You're not going anywhere."

"What do you mean?" I say.

"*You* are the show now."

r/TheUnderdog

Posted by Calming4ce_

Obsessed with Svetlana!!!

Everyone is so talented, but I literally felt GOD when she sang *Spirit Lead Me*.

Justin-Case97

i think shes gonna win

Calming4ce_

My bets on The Singing Patient. I watched the TikTok of her singing *Believe* at the psych hospital. I can't wait to see her perform tomorrow.

Justin-Case97

dude she's a fugitive now

Calming4ce_

WHAT???

Justin-Case97

she ran away at the airport

Calming4ce_

How?

Justin-Case97

heard she's rich and paid the show's chaperone to look the other way

Steffed_up

the chaperone says she wasn't paid off.

Calming4ce_

I'd definitely watch a show about THAT.

TEN
NORMA

One Year Earlier
July 2020

Norma approached the hospital, feeling a little shaky after drinking three cups of coffee earlier in the morning to help her stay awake. She had barely slept the night before, tossing and turning, feeling so disconnected from Cookie after their email exchange the night before.

Why had Cookie lied about being on bed rest? And was Liam really touring the maternity ward yesterday? Norma was about to try to get an answer to the second question.

She entered the hospital an hour before her volunteer shift was supposed to start and took the elevator upstairs, wearing the laminated volunteer badge with her name, which Jay had given her. She hoped not to run into him until her shift started. But if she did, she would pretend she had mixed up her start time.

She quickly exited the elevator and walked briskly down the hospital corridor to the room she'd seen Liam entering the day before. The door was closed. She looked both ways to ensure nobody was watching her before putting her ear on the door. She didn't hear anything until a baby cried out.

Norma couldn't help herself and swung the door open.

"Hi," a young woman said. She was lying in a hospital bed, cradling a baby girl with a pink beanie on her head.

"Hello," Norma said.

"Are you here to take her so I can rest?" the mother asked.

"Yes," Norma said, realizing the woman probably thought she was a nurse because of the badge around her neck.

"I'm Brooke," she said. "I was rushed to the hospital and left my glasses at home. I can't see your badge. What's your name?"

"Donna," Norma lied. She wasn't sure if she was allowed to be in a patient room in her volunteer capacity.

"This is Sadie," Brooke said, lovingly gazing at her baby girl.

"That's a beautiful name," Norma said.

"It was my Mom's name," Brooke said.

Norma remembered Cookie telling her that if Liam and she had a baby girl, they were going to name her Rose after Liam's Mom, who had passed away.

Norma knew she couldn't compete with a dead woman for her grandchild's first name. She had asked Cookie if they had settled on a middle name, thinking they had chosen Norma. But Cookie let her know they hadn't decided on one yet.

Norma remembered feeling hurt by the slight. There had been countless slights throughout Cookie's life. At first, they always stung sharply like a paper cut until the pain eventually faded. But over time, Norma noticed the pain didn't fade as easily. It mushroomed and metastasized. One paper cut after another. Death by a thousand paper cuts. And the one about Norma's future grandchild's middle name hung around Norma's neck like a noose.

"I know I have to rest," Brooke told Norma. "But it's really hard to part with her, even for a couple of hours. I wish my Mom were still alive and here with me now."

"I'm sorry," Norma said.

"Thanks," Brooke said. Her eyes watered.

"I'm sure your Mother would have given anything to be here too," Norma added.

"That's really kind of you," Brooke said.

Norma thought about Cookie, who had no idea how lucky she was to have a living parent ready to help her with a baby, and it made her burn inside.

Norma composed herself and reminded herself why she was there—to try to find out what Liam had been doing in this room the day before.

"I hope the expectant parent tours haven't been too disruptive for you," Norma said.

"Nobody's been by today since I delivered this morning," Brooke said.

"How about yesterday?" Norma asked.

"Just one tour right after I was admitted yesterday morning," Brooke said. "A guy was here on his own. He said his fiancé couldn't come because she was on bed rest."

So Liam had been touring the maternity ward. Norma wondered if he had convinced Cookie to deliver at Little Saint Mary's since he always got his way.

"I'm lucky I was spared bed rest during my pregnancy. It would've been hard on my husband, Anthony. He just stepped out for the first time to get some coffee," Brooke continued. "Smart man," Norma said. "He'll need a lot of coffee now. Sleepless nights are part of life with a newborn. You should rest while you can."

"I will," Brooke said, handing the baby girl to Norma.

As Norma took Sadie from Brooke, one of the girl's identification bracelets slipped off her ankle. Norma grabbed it just in time before it fell to the ground.

"My Mom told me I had a circulation problem when I was born," Brooke said. "I told my doctor and delivery team about it. They loosened Sadie's bracelets just in case."

"They did that and then some," Norma said, placing the bracelet back on Sadie's ankle.

"It's probably stupid," Brooke said near tears again. "She's a different person. I'm just grasping, trying to keep my Mom's memory alive. The longing never ends."

Norma gently put her hand on Brooke's shoulder.

"I lost my late husband," Norma told her. "Just because someone leaves us doesn't mean they're gone."

Brooke blinked away her tears.

Norma slipped out of the room with the baby girl, wondering if it was legal. Technically, she hadn't started her shift yet and wasn't sure if she was allowed to hold babies outside the nursery. Norma knew she needed to dispose of this child as soon as possible before anyone saw her, especially Jay.

She beelined to the nursery without anyone recognizing her. But when she stepped inside, her heart skipped a beat. A man was there in the corner of the room, talking on his cell phone. A potential witness to what she had done.

Norma played it cool as if she were supposed to be there. She found Sadie's crib by matching her ID bracelet name with the placard's name on Sadie's designated crib and placed her inside. She made sure the loosened ID bracelet was still on her ankle, along with the one on her wrist.

Norma looked over at the man, who seemed preoccupied. He was speaking loudly on a cell phone. "I tried fixing the camera, but it still isn't working. The red light won't turn on."

Norma hadn't even considered there was a camera in the nursery. When she looked up, she noticed two of them, one in each corner of the room.

"I checked the second camera too," the man continued. "It's not working either. I don't think this is a hardware issue. This morning, a big malware attack targeted multiple hospitals in the area. The backup system isn't working either. I need to contact the hospital cybersecurity unit..."

The man left his work bag in the corner of the room and walked out of the nursery, still talking on his phone. He didn't make eye contact with Norma, and she didn't think he noticed her. She was invisible to him like she was to Cookie, who had disposed of Norma like a used piece of Kleenex.

Norma stared at Sadie in the crib. She looked peaceful. The world was her oyster. Her entire life lay ahead of her.

Norma remembered looking at Cookie for the first time and thinking the same exact thing about her, and Norma's heart ached. She wasn't part of Cookie's life anymore. The chasm between them was growing with each passing day. In a few years' time, her daughter might not remember her at all.

NORMA WAS a couple of hours into her volunteer shift when she passed the nursery and spotted Liam again. He was back. But this time, he was inside of the nursery, standing next to a crib, staring at a baby.

What's he doing here again? Norma wondered.

She quickly walked the other way and waited by a nurse's station until Liam left the nursery. After, she casually returned and slipped inside. She approached the crib he had been standing by and gasped when she spotted the nameplate: **ROSE BUTTERFLY CASE.**

Cookie had delivered Norma's grandchild. Five days early—on the Fourth of July.

Norma remembered Cookie the day before, wincing and clutching her stomach after putting down her grocery bags. Maybe she had been on bed rest but defied doctors' orders and gone grocery shopping, which probably put her into labor. Norma knew better than anyone that Cookie was a very driven, Type A personality who had always had difficulty taking orders, no matter who was giving them, Liam being the only exception.

Norma stared at her granddaughter in the hospital crib and stared at her nameplate again. Cookie hadn't chosen Norma as Rose's middle name. Instead, she had chosen Butterfly, which wasn't even a real name.

Norma had to admit the name Rose seemed to suit her granddaughter, whose skin was rose-colored, similar to Sadie's. Rose looked remarkably like Sadie. If Norma hadn't known they had different parents, she might've mistaken the two baby girls for twins or, at the very least, that they had a father in common.

Do all babies look alike? Norma wondered.

It had been a long time since she'd been around infants. She looked around at the other babies in the hospital nursery cribs. They didn't all look alike. Some were ugly and had scrunched-up prune-like faces, even though they were brand new. Others had come out of the chute looking better, more angelic.

But Rose and Sadie looked a lot like. More than alike. Without their nameplates, Norma might've mistaken them for each other, and they were even born on the same day.

Norma wanted to pick up Rose and hold her more than anything. Her granddaughter was her legacy. The reason she had sacrificed her entire life for Cookie. But she knew she couldn't touch her. If Liam returned and saw Norma holding her, he might have her escorted out by security.

Tears formed in Norma's eyes. She worried she might break down and make a scene—or worse and more embarrassing, be recorded weeping inside the nursery with the hospital security watching her through their cameras.

She smiled tightly to push back the tears. It didn't work. A sob escaped her.

She looked up at the cameras in each corner of the room. The red lights the technician had spoken about on the phone earlier still weren't on. She noticed his bag was still in the corner. He had said the cameras weren't working. He also said the hospital backup system wasn't working due to that malware attack.

In all likelihood, Norma wasn't being recorded, so she let herself come apart. She wept for every hole left inside of her. The hole left by the daughter, who had abandoned her. The hole for the granddaughter she'd never know. The hole left by her late husband, who had died young on her. The hole left in the ashes of her unrealized dreams. The hole for a life that hadn't unfolded the way she had hoped for.

The urge to pick up Rose to comfort herself almost overtook Norma. She wanted to feel her flesh and blood. She *needed* to.

But she stopped herself and walked over to Sadie's crib

instead. She would hold the baby she was allowed to hold for comfort and not risk Liam or Cookie seeing her with Rose.

Before picking Sadie up, she made sure Sadie's loosened ID bracelet was still on her ankle when she noticed Sadie's foot looked *blue*. Brooke had mentioned a possible circulation issue. Norma wrapped her fingers around the foot. It was cold.

Norma stared at Sadie's chest, which didn't look like it was moving. She put her ear next to Sadie's mouth and didn't hear or feel her breath either.

Norma's stomach dropped.

Sadie was dead.

Norma thought of Brooke, who had lost her mom, a mom she had loved and desperately missed. And Norma knew she would never recover from this.

Norma thought about Cookie and her newborn Rose, who was cut from the same cloth as her mother. Who would model herself after Cookie. Norma knew Cookie would never survive the heartache Rose would inevitably cause her.

Norma knew what she needed to do. What any good mother would do for her daughter—protect Cookie.

Norma looked up again at the cameras in each corner of the nursery. The red lights still weren't on. She couldn't be one hundred percent she wasn't being recorded. But it didn't matter. Even if they were, she would be willing to face the consequences of her actions.

This was for Cookie. And Norma's entire life had been dedicated to her daughter.

Norma ran over to Rose's crib and used the sharp metal edge from her hospital volunteer badge clip to tear off Rose's identification bracelets from her wrist and ankle.

The crunching sound reminded Norma of stepping on a plastic water bottle before tossing it into the recycling bin. Turning something big and obscene and making it small to help restore order in the universe.

Norma swept up Rose without her identification bracelets and carried her to Sadie's crib. She slipped off Sadie's loosened bracelets, placing them on Rose's ankle and wrist, before carrying Sadie's lifeless body to Rose's crib.

She began administering CPR on Sadie in Rose's crib, the way Jay had taught to do it on the plastic doll the day before. When her efforts didn't work, she ran out of the nursery and called for help.

Nurses and doctors swept in, swarming Rose's crib like an army of ants surrounding a breadcrumb. They were doing everything in their power to valiantly revive Sadie, whom they called Rose.

Norma thought about how she would never have the chance to know her granddaughter. But she had no relationship with her, and she likely never would since Cookie had been brainwashed by a therapist.

The hope now was that in losing her daughter, Cookie would come to her senses, realize that Norma mattered, and return to her. Depending on the circumstances, Norma might consider giving Cookie a second chance.

The nursery had transformed into a scene of chaos. Machines were frantically rolled in. Monitors, defibrillators, and intravenous lines. Staff members were counting loudly with each chest compression as they administered CPR to Sadie, aka Rose, who was long gone.

Norma looked up at the television screen mounted in the corner of the nursery.

More chaos.

It was the Fourth of July 2020. Nobody was celebrating. Cities were burning. Protests, riots, and broken curfews were spreading like Malibu fires.

The universe was a cruel playground filled with wrongs that would never be righted.

Norma exhaled.

She finally felt a sense of peace.

With one small, brave gesture, she had made a correction.

ELEVEN
LIZ

Day Two
Sunday, July 4, 2021

It's July 4th, 2021. Last summer, the country was gripped in unrest. Several states had deployed the National Guard to their major cities, and many Fourth of July celebrations were canceled.

Now, a year later, festivities have returned. The Grove shopping center is having its annual Fourth of July celebration with music, food, and fireworks.

The Underdog chose to film its weekly singing competition here today with a makeshift stage near the water fountain. The contestants are on their way now. I'm meeting them and taking them to the stage for their sound check before tonight's show.

I almost didn't come to work today due to exhaustion. I barely slept last night, worried about what the police would uncover, even though I have nothing to do with Jennifer Addis's disappearance. Doug acted unusually nice to me yesterday due to my new infamy, and I probably have some leeway and might've been able to stay home. But I was worried if I didn't show up, it would make me look guilty. Like I don't need to work anymore because Jennifer Addis paid me off when she didn't.

After I got home last night, Erika, who got me the interview at *The Underdog*, reached out to see how I was doing. She had seen the news about Jennifer Addis's disappearance. Thankfully, she believed me when I told her I didn't know Jennifer. Erika suggested I contact the Directors Guild of America (DGA) for a pro-bono attorney referral. Their offices are closed today since it's Sunday and the Fourth of July. I'm planning to call first thing tomorrow morning.

I'm a DGA member due to a commercial I directed right after I graduated from AFI. I've kept up my membership through the years, paying small yearly dues of a couple hundred dollars, even when I was living out of my car, and even though I've never earned enough to qualify for the union health insurance.

Whenever I hold the shiny plastic guild membership card in my palm, I dream of being on set, directing my feature film adaptation of my second-chance romance short, *Moving On*. It's about a woman, Elle, who is going through a breakup and hires a mover, Stefan, to help her move from the luxury apartment she once shared with her ex-boyfriend to her new place. Stefan is kind and understanding and shares that he also went through a recent breakup.

As he loads up his van with her boxes, Elle notices and is bowled over by the graphic art painted on its exterior. Stefan explains he painted it himself. He helps people move to pay bills but hopes one day, his art will be enough to support him.

When Elle arrives at her new place and starts

unpacking each box, she's transported to another dimension where she's living the life she would have had with her ex if they hadn't broken up. On the outside, it appears enviable, filled with first-class jet-setting all over the world, staying at five-star hotels, owning multiple homes in dream locations, filled with every privilege imaginable. But on the inside, she's crumbling. Her ex is distant, and she's intensely lonely.

Elle quickly closes the boxes and, with them, the other dimension. She goes about her life for the next couple of months, too scared to open the boxes again, making do with what she already unpacked. Until one day, she decides it's time to open the boxes. This time, she isn't transported to another dimension, and her alternate life doesn't flash before her eyes. But she notices one of her boxes is missing.

She calls Stefan to ask if he forgot to unload it. He tells her he'll look for it. A day later, he arrives at her new apartment with the box and looks scared to give it to her. "I think we should open it together," he says.

"Okay," she says, confused.

Stefan stands next to Elle as she opens the cardboard flaps. Once again, she's transported into another dimension. But this time, to her surprise, she's living out her happily ever after with him—the mover!

Money is scarce, but they get by, and she is happy—happier than she's ever been in her life, until two years later when Stefan tragically dies in a car accident during a moving job. The gaping hole of grief inside of her is unending. A life without him feels unimaginable. She also knows love, like what they had, is unlikely to strike twice in a lifetime.

Elle plans his memorial and decides to showcase Stefan's art as a tribute to him. Someone takes a picture of one of his pieces, posts it on social media, and *Art News* picks up the story. They share Stefan's pieces from his memorial service and a picture of him standing in front of his van that he painted. The story and his art go viral.

Strangers start flooding Elle with requests to purchase Stefan's work. Museum curators from top modern art museums all over the world contact her, requesting to do exhibits featuring it. Stefan is experiencing the attention and success for his art that eluded him in life, and Elle is now entrusted with it.

Elle shuts the moving box's flaps and, with it, the other dimension. She looks at Stefan, and he looks at her as we fade to black. The viewer is left wondering what happens next. Will Elle move forward with Stefan, knowing her second chance at love may be short-lived? Will Stefan move forward with Elle, knowing death is possibly imminent and he'll never experience success as an artist while alive? The audience is left asking what they would do if they were in either of their shoes.

Five years ago, I almost got the chance to turn *Moving On* into a feature when I met with Erika's then-husband, Paul, who had just inherited a life-changing amount of money. He was looking for artists to sponsor, and Erika, who has always believed in my talent since I took her AFI cinematography class, suggested I meet with him to pitch my feature.

We met for lunch at The Ivy on Robertson. He said he had seen my short and was very impressed. He listened attentively as I made my case for why the world needs romcoms now more than ever. "We need to believe love still exists, and one way to do that is by asking ourselves what we'd be willing to sacrifice for love."

Maybe it's because I needed to believe love still existed after my marriage fell apart.

Paul offered me two hundred thousand dollars. A bare-bones budget for a feature, but I knew I could make it work with contacts from AFI who would help me.

Joyful is an understatement for how I felt. My dream was finally about to come true. The years of struggle and hardship had all been worth it. Until Paul told me the price attached: sleep with him.

I was shocked and devastated. I quickly turned him down and bolted out of the restaurant. Later, Erika told me Paul didn't think my film was the right fit for him to produce. I didn't know what to do. I didn't want to be the one responsible for possibly ruining her marriage. But in the end, I decided that if it were me, I would've wanted to know the truth and told her. She thanked me, and our conversation ended cordially.

I didn't know if I'd hear from her again. But I did six months later when she called me to let me know she had gotten a divorce. She reassured me I wasn't to blame me, and I thanked her for reaching out.

Last night, I was grateful for her call and support. My two roommates were also supportive after learning what had happened online. They were as much intrigued as sympathetic to my plight and helped me do a deep-dive search into The Singing Patient online.

Stefanie is a make-up artist obsessed with Reddit, and Vince is a computer programmer. They took me down several online conspiracy rabbit holes about Jennifer Addis. But nothing turned up to help clarify why she ran away, if she paid off my student loans, or where she might be right now.

I need to find her. She's the only one who can clear my

name by letting the police know that I have nothing to do with her disappearance.

I tossed and turned all night, terrified. I thought about the last nine years of my life and every decision I've made since I graduated from AFI, which has brought me to this moment.

Several former AFI classmates went on to have big careers, including my nemesis, Emily, who hooked up with my then-AFI boyfriend, Tommy, while we were all still in school together. She became one of the first female directors Blumhouse hired to shoot a Manga-inspired horror film.

The last time I looked her up, I saw an Architectural Digest spread of her and Tommy's Mid-Century Modern masterpiece home with their bulldogs dressed in matching pink cotton candy-colored hoodies sitting in front of a heated pool with views of the Hollywood sign.

At the time, I was living out of my car. Seeing that they were still together, basking in the glory of all of their success, stung. Unlike Emily, I've never stolen anyone's boyfriend, yet I was the one struggling and without a career.

Not all of the graduates from my AFI year made it. Some left LA, returned to their hometowns, and forged lives unrelated to the entertainment business, like the one I had before I got divorced. I learned about them through social media. Eventually, I hid and muted their profiles from my feeds. Even though they hadn't made it, they had real lives, unlike my aspirational one. The comparison game was too painful.

Maybe I should've asked Dad for help and moved back in with him until I got back on my feet as a physical thera- pist. But there's always been an unflappable corner deep inside of me that's unwilling to give up. That still believes I can make it as a director. Maybe because of what happened with my ex-husband.

I had shared my dreams about becoming a director with him. He always acted supportive in front of me, but his computer told an entirely different story. We were planning a vacation, and one day while he was at work, I went to look up his mileage plus number on his desktop to book our airplane tickets. A message thread was opened with one of his friends making fun of me.

He texted his buddy: **She thinks she's the next Jordan Peele** with an eye roll emoji.

Wannabe, his friend texted back with a laughter tears emoji.

I scrolled up, and there were many months of messages disparaging me. To read streams worth of texts ridiculing and belittling me was an excruciatingly painful betrayal.

After, I told him I wanted a divorce and explained why. He didn't fight me. I left the marriage with a shattered heart and an even more shattered self-esteem.

It took a lot of strength to chase my dream in the face of knowing the person who was supposed to have my back had mocked me for it. But I still went for it. Maybe that's why I've never been able to quit. I don't want to believe he was right. That I'm just a wannabe.

The shuttle bus with the contestants pulls into the parking lot. I greet them as they file out, one by one.

Svetlana uses her fake walking stick and pretends to clumsily disembark the steps with the bus driver's help. Our eyes meet through her sunglasses, and she smiles at me.

"Hi, Svetlana," I say.

She brushes past me, moves her mouth close to my ear, and whispers, "Didn't think you had it in you."

TWELVE

NORMA

Day Two
Sunday, July 4, 2021

Norma sat on a crowded shuttle bus, clutching a hidden bottle of Mace pepper spray in the embroidered pocket of her prairie dress. She was on her way to The Grove shopping center in Los Angeles.

One year had passed since she had spotted Rose in the hospital nursery and switched her with a dead Sadie. After, she quit her volunteer job, citing the grief of losing her granddaughter. The staff was very sympathetic. Jay told her that her position would be waiting for her if she ever decided to return. A medical examiner later concluded Rose, aka Sadie, had died of SIDS.

Norma had gotten away with it. Nobody had seen her switching the babies, and she hadn't been recorded. But after that, things didn't go according to her plan. A couple of weeks after Rose's supposed death, Cookie still hadn't reached out to Norma.

Norma drove by Cookie and Liam's house to see if she

might run into her daughter and find out how she was doing. Instead, Norma saw a FOR SALE sign in the front yard. She wondered where Cookie was moving to but couldn't ask. Norma called Cookie's job to try to get information, pretending she needed to speak with Cookie about a work-related matter. She was informed that Cookie had gone on an indefinite leave.

Norma followed Cookie's house sale closely, regularly driving by the home until the sale closed. Shortly after a new family moved in, Norma contacted the P.I. she had hired to take pictures of Liam with the actress to see if the detective could find out where Cookie had moved to. He found Cookie and Liam's new rental address, which was local, and gave it to Norma. She drove by the new house and saw Liam in front, who didn't see her.

She tried going by several more times, hoping to run into Cookie, but she never saw her. The final time, Liam noticed Norma parked in her car down the street and ran up to her. He pounded on her window and shouted, "Leave us alone!"

"I just want to know how Cookie is doing," Norma said through the car window's glass.

"I'm filing a restraining order against you right now," Liam said, pulling out his phone. Norma quickly drove away before any officer arrived. She wanted to reach out to the Mothers of Estranged Daughters Facebook group for support. But she had stopped participating because she couldn't share with the other members what she had done.

Sometimes, Norma felt guilty about switching the babies. But it wasn't like she could go to the police and tell them what she had done. She knew she had committed a crime, even though it was to spare Cookie a lifetime of having a daughter like her. However, the courts, like the

Facebook group, would never understand Norma's reasoning.

The last time Norma logged onto Facebook, the actor Keanu Reeves had contacted her, or so she thought. He told her he liked older women, and they spent a month messaging each other. One day, he messaged her that he wanted to meet in person, but she first needed her to transfer money into his bank account.

This struck Norma as odd because he was a famous actor who had made millions in the movie business. But he explained that he was down on his luck due to a few bad investments. Still, Norma's spidey senses were triggered and confirmed when, shortly after, two more Keanu Reeves contacted her—Keanu2301 and Keanu_45, wanting to start a relationship with an older woman. Then, three different "Elon Musks" reached out. She sent the original conman a message, telling him to leave her alone, and closed up the app for good.

Days turned into weeks, and weeks turned into months. Loneliness overtook Norma like a blanket of thick, heavy mud. All she was left with in the world was her pet stuffed monkey, Oreo, who wasn't technically hers. Cookie had won him in a fair when she was seven years old.

After she left for college, she abandoned Oreo just like she had abandoned Norma, and Norma inherited him. When Cookie returned home for her first summer break, she saw Norma had moved Oreo from her bedroom to the living room couch.

"You're turning into Norma Desmond from *Sunset Boulevard*," she told Norma, laughing. Cookie always had a salty side.

The truth was Oreo had helped lessen Norma's loneliness. But Norma didn't tell Cookie that. Instead, she reminded Cookie that Oreo was a stuffed monkey, unlike the real one that Norma Desmond had buried in the film.

Now, Oreo wasn't enough to shake the blanket of despair that had enveloped Norma after being abandoned again by Cookie. Daily tasks like going to the supermarket, paying bills, and cleaning the house became impossible. Dishes piled up in the sink. Garbage overflowed in the kitchen trash can.

When Norma ran out of groceries and stopped eating for a few days, she fainted. After she came to, her cheek plastered on the laminate kitchen floor, she started ordering food to be delivered to her home to avoid having to go to the market.

Once, she passed out on the living room couch and didn't have the energy to walk to the bathroom. When she finally couldn't hold it in for another second, she got up but didn't make it in time and relieved herself on Cookie's bedroom carpet instead. It was the only thing that had made Norma feel mildly good in months.

But two weeks ago, everything changed on a dime for Norma. She had sat on the couch next to Oreo to get her nightly fix of television when the blind Ukrainian orphan reappeared on her television screen.

It had been about a year since Norma had seen the girl on *Dateline*. Now, she discovered that Svetlana was a contestant on a new singing show called *The Underdog*.

The show aired a video montage of Svetlana's backstory, including the *Dateline* episode featuring her singing at the Boys and Girls Club. A producer who had watched the episode a year prior remembered her performance and recruited her.

Norma watched Svetlana perform *Spirit Lead Me* again. This time, to a rousing standing ovation from *The*

Underdog's audience members and judges. She felt a sudden burst of energy. Something she hadn't felt in close to a year.

Because Norma and Svetlana had a connection, even if Svetlana didn't know it yet. They had both been abandoned by people who were supposed to love them.

Norma decided to plan a trip to visit Svetlana on the show, which was filmed in Los Angeles. She planned to explain to Svetlana how she had been abandoned too—by Cookie—and offer to take the poor orphan in since she had the money and the room.

After several failed attempts to purchase an airline ticket online, Norma went to a local Triple AAA office to meet with a travel agent to help her book a flight. When she walked through the parking lot on her way inside, she noticed a man in a baseball cap standing by a large SUV with his face down. When she left the office with her plane ticket booked, she noticed he was still there—now, closer to her car.

She wondered if he had been following her. She quickly got inside her car and drove away. It unnerved her enough that she went to a hardware store to purchase a bottle of the Mace pepper spray, which she started carrying around. She decided to pack it for her trip to Los Angeles since this was her first time traveling alone.

Now, she was seated on a crowded shuttle bus in LA on her way to meet Svetlana, clutching the Mace bottle inside her pocket. She looked around at the tourist families and thought back to the last time she had traveled to the city of angels when she had the protection of a man. In her early twenties, Norma's mother had watched Cookie while Norma's late husband, Ray, and she went on a belated honeymoon trip.

Norma smiled, thinking about how they had taken in the sights and sounds of Hollywood while riding double-decker buses throughout the city. Ray died unexpectedly of a heart attack a few years later, leaving Norma a house and enough money not to have to work. He wasn't a perfect husband, but he was a good man.

She had missed him through the years, especially when Cookie acted up during her adolescence. Even with resources, being a single parent had not been easy, especially with a daughter like Cookie.

The shuttle bus pulled into the Grove shopping center, and everyone filed out. They had one hour until the show started. Norma was hungry and went to Du-Par's pie shop to get a slice of Key Lime pie. It was the best slice of Key Lime she had ever tasted. Norma wished she had someone to share it with. Maybe, soon, she would share one with Svetlana.

After she finished eating, she returned to the stage in the middle of the shopping center and took a seat when she spotted Svetlana standing with a group of contestants behind a red velvet rope.

Norma had thought a lot about what she would say to the orphan and decided to speak from her heart. She got up from her chair and approached Svetlana, who was wearing sunglasses and using a walking stick.

"Hi, I'm Norma. You have a beautiful voice," she said.

"Thank you," Svetlana said with a slight accent.

"I'm a big fan. I've followed your story since *Dateline*, and I want you to know I never would've abandoned you."

Svetlana nodded her head.

"Nobody deserves to be abandoned by their family," Norma continued.

Svetlana awkwardly smiled.

"My daughter, Cookie, abandoned me too," Norma said. "You and I have a lot in common."

Svetlana started to inch away from Norma using her walking stick.

What's she doing? Norma wondered.

THIRTEEN
LIZ

Day Two
Sunday, July 4, 2021

"I know everyone is disappointed that The Singing Patient isn't here, but we still have an amazing line-up tonight," C.J. announces.

C.J. is twenty-five, has a YouTube channel and a hit show, and was hired to be *The Underdog's* announcer because the producers thought he might help attract Gen Z eyeballs.

He's standing on the stage, speaking. The contestants are below, lined up behind a red velvet rope, waiting for C.J. to call them up to perform.

A strange, older-looking woman is talking to Svetlana. Svetlana starts backing away from her uncomfortably. I wonder if she knows her or whether I need to get security involved.

I walk up to Svetlana. The woman sees me, walks away, and returns to her seat. "Are you okay?" I ask Svetlana.

"Yeah," Svetlana says. "I think she might be an obsessed fan."

"I'll ask security to stand over here for the rest of the show," I say.

"Thanks," Svetlana says.

"Let me know if you need someone to walk with to the shuttle bus after," I say.

"Are you reeeeady?" C.J.'s voice thunders from the stage.

I walk away from Svetlana, locate a security guard, and explain the situation to him. He walks over to the red velvet rope and positions himself next to her.

Doug texts me that he has just arrived to watch the show. I text him back and let him know what happened with Svetlana and that security is covering her now.

C.J. keeps talking from the stage. He announces the first performer, Winnie, a nineties actress who was caught shoplifting one too many times. She walks up to the stage and sings *Redemption Song* by Bob Marley while playing the guitar. Everyone is entranced.

The rest of the performances go just as well, including Svetlana's stirring cover of *Rise Up*, which brings the entire audience and judges to their feet.

When the show ends, C.J. returns to the stage. "Thanks again to all of our contestants for another incredible night. Please make sure to vote and tune in on Tuesday night for the elimination results—" He suddenly stops speaking and stares at the teleprompter. "It looks like we have one more unexpected performance... The Singing Patient!"

The audience gasps. The stage goes dark, except for the large projector screen behind it, on which Jennifer appears.

She's standing in a nondescript room by a window with

a mic. There's a single overhead light above her and a picture of her daughter taped to the wall behind her.

She starts singing *I Won't Back Down* by Tom Petty, a cappella. As the first word comes out of her mouth, it's clear she's holding back tears. She keeps singing through her pain until she gets to the part about being at the gates of hell and refusing to back down. She closes her eyes, touches the picture behind her of her daughter, and no longer holds back. Tears run down her cheeks like rain tracks down a window pane.

Her despair and longing for her child are visceral. The performance is nothing short of astonishing. After her final note, the light above her turns off, and the projector screen goes black on the makeshift stage. For a brief second, the judges and audience sit silently in awe until everyone bursts into a standing ovation that won't let up.

"The Singing Patient!" C.J. roars as he walks back onto the stage.

I pull out my phone, scanning every social media account for *The Underdog*. Maybe someone on the internet picked up where Jennifer filmed her performance—a possible clue that might help me locate her.

But all the social media comments are about her performance:

Oh, she's a STAR'S star....

Literal goosebumps!!!

That is the ONLY version I ever wanna hear again.

Doug runs up to me. I've never seen him this excited before. "Can you believe it!?" he says.

"Do you know where she is?" I ask.

"No, I heard she sent a video attachment of the performance through a random email," he says.

I bite down on my lip, worried. She's so close, yet so far away. I'm no closer to finding her so she can clear me of involvement with her disappearance.

I look over at Doug, who is beaming and couldn't care less about my troubles.

"Our ratings are going to be fire," he says.

r/TheUnderdog
Posted by Calming4ce_
The Singing Patient!!!

HOLY FUCK!

Steffed_up
she has a great voice.

Justin-Case97
i think she's gonna win

Calming4ce_
If she can perform again…looked like she was in witness
protection.

Justin-Case97
what did she mean about not backing down

Calming4ce_
Maybe that she won't back down from fighting for her daughter,
did anyone else notice the baby picture behind her?

Steffed_up
i did.

Justin-Case97
whats the deal with her husband

Steffed_up
i heard he was against her doing the show.

Calming4ce_

If my wife had a voice like that, I'd ask her to sing all the time.

Justin-Case97

it's kinda weird he's mia

FOURTEEN

NORMA

Day Two
Sunday, July 4, 2021

Norma took a taxi back to her motel, feeling defeated. Everyone was starry-eyed and obsessed with The Singing Patient's surprise performance, but all Norma could think about was Svetlana.

Norma had tried approaching her again during a commercial break to tell her how incredible she thought her performance of *Rise Up* was. But Svetlana told Norma in no uncertain terms to leave her alone. A security guard standing nearby warned Norma that he would escort her out of the shopping center if she didn't stay seated.

Norma wished she had never traveled to Los Angeles to meet Svetlana.

She had done it out of the goodness of her heart. She had even left Oreo behind alone. She hadn't packed him out of fear that the airline might lose her luggage.

No good deed goes unpunished.

Norma walked up the flight of stairs of the Elvis-inspired motel. Back in the day, she loved The King with his soulful voice and powerful moves. Each guest room in the motel had metallic gold and silver finishes in a nod to him.

The motel also had a pool in the shape of a piano. The July weather was warm enough for Norma to take a night dip, but she was too upset to swim.

She reached the second floor and walked toward her guest room. It was dark out, and she clutched the bottle of Mace pepper spray in her pocket. She was glad to have it because she noticed the motel had no cameras. A regular hotel probably would've had them, but Norma chose this motel because of Elvis. In hindsight, it might have been an unwise choice because nobody would know if anything happened to her.

But would anyone even care if something happened to me? she wondered.

She passed a few rooms when one of the doors swung open. She gasped when she saw who was standing there.

"Liam," Norma said, surprised. "What are you doing here?"

"Come in," he said, smiling.

"Is Cookie with you?" Norma asked. She stepped inside and looked for her, but Cookie wasn't there.

Liam shut the door and turned around to face Norma.

"I know what you did," he said, dropping his smile.

"What do you mean?" Norma asked, confused.

"I saw you at Little Saint Mary's the day before Rose was born when I was touring the maternity ward. Cookie told me you were volunteering there. You were probably scheming how to carry out your twisted plan the entire time."

"What are you talking about?" Norma said.

"You stole our daughter and gave her to someone else," he said.

"I did no such thing," Norma said.

"Yes, you did because you're a psychopath," Liam said, inching towards her.

"They don't let psychopaths volunteer at hospitals." Norma chuckled defensively. "I know how grief-stricken you and Cookie must be over losing Rose, but I had nothing to do—"

"Do <u>NOT</u> say my daughter's name!" Liam shouted, interrupting Norma. "That was my birth mother's name, who I never got to know because, by the time I found out who my biological parents were, they were both dead."

"I'm sorry to hear that," Norma said.

"When I learned I was going to be a dad, it was the happiest moment of my life," Liam said, ignoring her. "And you stole it from me. You would've gotten away with it if I hadn't been registered with Ancestry.com to find my biological parents. The problem for you is that Rose has a rare genetic disorder. When the parents you gave her to ran tests to find out if they had other relatives with it on Ancestry, they discovered they weren't her real parents and that I'm her Dad."

Norma started to feel nervous and tried reassuring herself that the hospital must not have any proof she was involved with the switch, or they would've contacted her by now. The best thing she could do was maintain that she was innocent.

"I don't know anything about this. I swear—" she said.

"BULLSHIT!" Liam screamed.

Norma jumped back, fearful, glad to have the pepper spray in her pocket.

"The girls were switched!" he yelled. "The parents

contacted the hospital to tell them the baby they brought home wasn't theirs and found out I had a child born on the same day as their daughter, who died. Now, they don't want to give up Rose without a legal fight."

Norma was happy to hear this news. She didn't think Liam would make a good father. He certainly had a rageful streak. Brooke seemed like a good mom when Norma briefly met her, unlike Cookie, who would have had no clue how to be a good mother to Rose, considering she had abandoned Norma.

"I don't know how you did it," Liam continued. "I've been following you everywhere, including to the Triple AAA office when you booked your flight here."

Norma remembered the man she had seen in the parking lot office. The one she had thought might have been following her. She now realized it was Liam.

"Why did you follow me?" Norma asked.

"To figure it out how you did. I still haven't, but the hospital through their investigation with the police will."

"You're mixed up right now," Norma said. "An egregious medical error must have happened that doesn't involve me. Once they come to that conclusion, I expect you to apologize."

"Apologize for what YOU did, you crazy stalker bitch?" Liam said. He pulled out a gun hidden underneath his shirt behind his pant belt. He could only see red.

Norma froze.

She now noticed an unusually large suitcase behind him. Large enough to fit a human body. Norma realized Liam had hit a point of no return. She needed to bring him back to reality.

"I swear I had nothing to do with what happened to Rose. Please don't do anything you'll regret. I know

Cookie doesn't want to be in touch with me, but I'm sure she doesn't want me dead, either, especially at your hands."

"How the fuck do you know what she wants?" Liam said, approaching Norma. He pointed the gun right at her.

"I'm her mother," Norma said.

"A mother only in name," he whispered. "I care more about her than you ever will. I nursed her broken heart for the last year after she thought Rose had died. She stopped working. We lost our house. I haven't told her about any of this yet because I don't want to break her heart again since we're now staring down a legal fight to get our daughter back. At least when she finds out, she'll never have to see your face again."

Liam threw down the gun on the metallic gold Elvis-inspired comforter and launched at Norma, pinning her down on the ground.

Norma's head landed with a heavy thud on the motel carpet. She screamed and tried fighting him off. He quickly put his hands around her neck, squeezing tightly, quieting her down.

Norma felt the air leaving her chest. She tried lifting her arms to push Liam's hands off her neck, but her arms went numb. They felt weightless. She was losing oxygen quickly and wondered if this was the end of her run.

Her tingling fingers grazed her dress pocket when she felt the outline of the *bottle of Mace pepper spray*. She needed to get it out, but she was slipping in and out of consciousness.

During one singular lucid moment, she mustered all of her remaining strength to maneuver her hand inside the embroidered patch pocket. She reached for the spray, lifted the bottle, and showered Liam's eyes.

His hands immediately fell from her neck, and he recoiled backward.

"What the fuck?" he said. He was now bent on the ground, covering his red, inflamed, burning eyes with his hands.

Norma coughed uncontrollably, gasping, choking, and gulping for air. She stood up and nearly tumbled over because she was overcome with dizziness.

She tried to make her way to the bed to grab Liam's gun since he was still on the ground, blinded by the pepper spray. She almost reached it when Liam grabbed one of her ankles, sliding her back to him, inch by sorry inch.

Norma slid by a side table with an ice bucket filled with melted ice water and an ice pick. She grabbed the pick as Liam kept pulling her from behind.

She knew from the *Dateline* episode about the ice pick serial killer that sticking it in Liam's neck might kill him, and she didn't want to kill him. She wasn't a murderer. She just wanted to get him off of her and get out of the motel room to call the police for help. "You're going to sleep for good," he said ominously. He kept pulling her from behind when Norma surprised him. She suddenly turned around and crammed the ice pick into his left eye socket.

Liam howled like a lone wolf howling at the moon. He let go of Norma's ankle and placed his hands on the ice pick, trying to dislodge it from his eyeball when his body started to convulse uncontrollably. He fell flat on the ground, shaking and foaming at the mouth before going completely still.

Norma approached him, scared he might attack her again, like the bad guy in the movies who was dead and then alive again.

"Liam?" Norma asked.

He didn't respond.

She noticed his chest wasn't moving. She carefully walked up closer and picked up his limp wrist. He had no pulse.

Norma stared at his lifeless body in disbelief. All she had ever tried to do was protect Cookie.

Now look where it got her.

She had killed a man.

FIFTEEN

LIZ

Day Two
Sunday, July 4, 2021

I just blew through a red light accidentally. Jennifer Addis's performance shook me. She felt so close. Like I could touch her. But I still have no way of reaching her.

I think there was a camera at the intersection when I went through the red, which means I have a big ticket coming my way for a moving violation. My insurance premiums will also go up. Like I can afford either.

I'M BACK at my apartment, sitting on the couch with my roommates. They watched The Singing Patient's performance. The entire country did.

"She might've been in a hotel room," Stefanie says.

"She can't go to a hotel," Vince says. "People would recognize her there."

"Not if she's wearing a mask," Stefanie says.

My phone makes a sound. I pick it up from the coffee table. It's an email with the subject line: **AIRPORT FOOTAGE.**

I open and read it:

Make a 100K payment to LUCKYLIZ$$ PayPal account in the next 24 hours, or this video will be sent to TMZ / police.

There's a link underneath.

"Don't click on it," Vince says. "It's probably a phishing scam."

"I need to know what it is," I say.

I press play before either of them can stop me. The three of us huddle on the couch, watching footage of me standing outside the airport bathroom. It was right after I realized Jennifer Addis wasn't in her stall. When I ran out, scanning the Hudson bookstore, Starbucks, and the Grill restaurant to see if she was there. In the video, she runs out of the bathroom *after* I'm outside, and I turn my head in the opposite direction. But that never happened. She was long gone when I ran out, and I turned my head in multiple directions while searching for her. Someone spliced this to make it look like we were both there at the same time. It's easy to merge two video files. You don't need to go to film school for that. All you need is the right software and an iPhone.

Panic flushes through me like an iodine fluid contrast material before a C.T. scan. A brief warm sensation followed by a funny taste in my mouth.

"This was manipulated!" I say. "Some stranger must've been at the airport filming and cut this to make it seem like I was in front of the bathroom before she ran out and that I deliberately looked away from her. But by the time I exited the bathroom, she was long gone.

Vince is on his phone now. "Check this out," he says, pointing to a picture of Rihanna at the same United terminal at JFK. "Rihanna was there the same day as you, which means paparazzi were there too, who are now trying to make a buck off you."

"I don't have 100k," I say, holding back tears. "They said they'll release it in the next twenty-four hours. Everyone's already running with the narrative that I'm guilty."

"You're contacting the DGA tomorrow for a lawyer referral, right?" Vince says.

"First thing," I say. "But attorneys aren't detectives. They won't be able to help me find Jennifer Addis. She's the only one who can clear my name."

SIXTEEN

NORMA

Day Two
Sunday, July 4, 2021

Norma stepped over Liam's body to get to the motel door. She moved the DO NOT DISTURB SIGN from the inside to the outside before closing and locking it.

She walked over to the unusually large suitcase and unzipped it. Inside were a backpack, Hefty trash bags, latex gloves, and a few gallons of Clorox bleach.

Premeditated, Norma thought.

She had been a dead woman walking and hadn't even known it.

Liam had planned this. He had stalked her and learned about her trip to Los Angeles at the Triple AAA office. He had followed her all the way here to do away with her in the City of Angeles.

He was a *bad man.*

Norma had never wanted to kill him, but if she had had to kill someone, she was glad it was him. He was going to kill her in cold blood, and there was no doubt that the world and Cookie were better off with him gone.

Norma had watched enough *Dateline* episodes to know killers used bleach to destroy DNA, and she needed to remove all of her DNA from his motel room. Thankfully, if there was one thing Norma had perfected in the decades of raising Cookie, it was cleaning.

She got to work, put on the latex gloves, took a towel from the motel bathroom, soaked it with bleach, and used it to wipe down the ice pick she had stuck in Liam's eyeball. She wiped down Liam's hands, which he'd wrapped around her neck. She removed his wallet from his pocket to make it look like a robbery before dumping the rest of the bleach all over the ground, especially on the area where he had pinned her down.

She looked out the door's peephole and saw nobody was there. She grabbed the bleach-drenched towel, slung it over her neck, opened the door, and quickly returned to her room.

Norma took off the latex gloves and placed them in a ziplock bag in her suitcase along with Liam's wallet. She would bring both back home and get rid of them there.

Now, she needed to destroy any traces of Liam's DNA left on her body. Norma knew from the chemistry class she had taken in college, when she still believed she could become a doctor, that pool-grade chlorine and a jug of Clorox were essentially the same thing, albeit with different concentrations, but certainly enough to degrade DNA.

She slipped on her pop pink high-neck one-piece swimsuit and headed downstairs to the Elvis-inspired pool, with the towel from Liam's motel room still draped around her neck.

Norma approached the piano-shaped pool and stuck her big left toe in the water, twirling it around. The water felt a little cold. She inhaled the scent of chlorine before dropping the towel from her neck into the pool, and then dove in.

SEVENTEEN

LIZ

Day Three
Monday, July 5, 2021

"I never met Jennifer Addis until I picked her up at the psychiatric hospital yesterday," I tell Jeff Abrams.

I told him the same thing on the phone this morning after I got his contact information from the directors' guild when I called their offices for attorney referrals. They told me he offered reduced rates to DGA members.

He agreed to meet me at his office in Mid-Wilshire after I explained it was an emergency and said he wouldn't charge me for this consultation. "Let's back up," he says. "Have you verified that your student loans were paid off?"

"Yes," I say. "I called Fanny Mae and also checked online. If Jennifer Addis paid them off, the only reason I can come up with is that she feels sorry for leaving me in this shit storm. But it just makes me look guilty. Like she paid me off to help her escape. The detective I met with at JFK said that if they can connect me to her disappearance, I'll be charged for helping a fugitive to escape."

"While she is considered a fugitive because she fled a psychiatric hospital," Jeff says. "They haven't connected you to anything yet. They'll need to establish prior communication between you two through emails, call logs, and testimonies from people who could corroborate that you helped her. They don't have a case if they can't do that."

"Someone's trying to extort me now with a manipulated video. Creating fake emails and call logs seems like it would be just as easy to do," I say. "Look at this email I got last night." I pull out my phone and play the airport footage for him. "Whoever sent this threatened to share it with TMZ and the police unless I make a PayPal payment to them for 100k by the end of day."

"I need the PayPal email address they provide you," Jeff says while typing on his computer. "And you need to report this to the NYPD immediately. We also need to get ahead of it and release a statement explaining you're being extorted because it could happen again."

"I feel like I've already lost the public," I say, near tears. "People are already running with the narrative that she paid me off."

"You haven't lost anything," he says. "And I'll do everything I can to ensure it stays that way. Ten percent of my practice is dedicated to pro-bono cases. I just finished one up and can take your case on."

I'm unsure if this is benevolence on his part or if he thinks my case will be good exposure for his practice since it's high-profile. Either way, I'm grateful because I need his help.

"This isn't the kind of case I normally take on," he says. "I don't like being in the limelight, but I know you're going through a lot. The DGA cases I've worked on in the past mainly involve ensuring directors are paid fairly by the streamers and studios."

I wish I were here to get my fair due as a director.

"Maybe one day I'll be able to hire you for that," I say. "I went to AFI for directing."

"Great school," he says.

I want to tell him about my short, how it was almost nominated for an Oscar, and my dream of turning it into a feature film one day. But I feel silly bringing it up since it was years ago and in light of where I find myself now.

"It was," I say.

"I know how tough it is to get work in any creative field," he says. "But it's important work. The world needs more artists now."

I could cry. No guy, except for Dad, has ever said anything this supportive to me about my artistic dreams.

Jeff smiles at me, a warm smile. His kind brown eyes sparkle.

"Thanks," I say.

"Life's too short not to chase your dreams," he says. "Most of my pro-bono cases are fighting insurance companies to pay medical claims. My Mom and Dad had to divorce before my Dad died because they were going bankrupt when their insurance carrier refused to pay for his cancer treatments. The only way they could protect her from bankruptcy and ensure she wouldn't inherit his medical debt was to divorce before he died. They had been married thirty-nine years."

"I'm sorry," I say.

He nods his head. "Thank you," he says.

I feel terrible for him. It's such a sad story. Yet he found a way to do something good because of it. He works pro bono fighting the bad guys.

This is the nice Jewish boy I'm sure Mom would've loved for me to end up with. She was killed in a car accident shortly after my bat mitzvah, a right-of-passage ceremony for Jewish teenagers. I remember how proud she looked during the ceremony, smiling at me as I stood on the temple's bema, reciting my Torah portion. I've always been thankful she lived long enough to be there for it. Sadly, after she died, our family's traditions, including religious ones, seemed to go by the wayside.

Jeff is smart, good-looking, and seems like a decent person. In another life and under other circumstances, maybe something would've been possible between us, assuming he even would've been interested in me in that way. It's probably just my romcom brain talking.

The truth is I haven't dated anyone since Tommy, my former AFI boyfriend, who hooked up with Emily. And he was the only guy I dated after my marriage ended. It's been hard to open up my heart again.

Even though I still believe in myself, sometimes my ex-husband gets in my head. What if he was right? What if I'm just a wannabe? A joke. A loser. Given the situation I find myself in now, I can't help but wonder if he was right. And who would want to be with someone like that?

Jeff's cell phone makes a sound. He lifts it from his desk and glances at it.

"Shit," he says.

"What happened?" I ask.

"Unfortunately, our problems just got bigger," he says.

"What do you mean?" I say.

"Jennifer Addis's husband is dead."

EIGHTEEN

NORMA

Day Three
Monday, July 5, 2021

Norma debated checking out of the motel after the ugly scene in Liam's room. But she thought leaving late at night would make her look suspicious, so she returned to her room after the dip in the piano-shaped pool and stayed put.

She didn't sleep much, wondering if anyone had heard Liam and her fighting in his room, and called the motel staff or police. She peeked out the window at least a dozen times, but the motel remained quiet overnight.

When the sun began to rise, Norma got ready. She went to the bathroom, looked in the mirror, and noticed bruises around her neck in the shape of Liam's fingerprints. She used make-up foundation to cover them and wrapped a breezy summer scarf around her neck for good measure.

Afterward, she headed downstairs to eat the complimentary breakfast included in her reservation. She sat at a table, drinking orange juice and coffee, and ate a surprisingly moist mini blueberry muffin. When she got up to get another muffin, she heard a couple at an adjacent table talking about *The Underdog*.

"The Singing Patient was amazing, but I'm rooting for the orphan. I feel so sorry for her," the woman said.

Norma's lip curled in disgust. Because of what had happened with Liam, she had temporarily forgotten what Svetlana had done to her. She knew she probably shouldn't draw attention to herself by saying anything to the couple, but she couldn't help herself.

"While the orphan may be an orphan, she's not a good person," Norma announced to them.

The woman was chewing a bite of scrambled eggs, and the man was sipping his coffee. They both looked up at Norma, surprised.

"I flew in to see her perform, and she was rude to me," Norma added.

"That's awful," the woman said. "I'm sorry."

"Thank you," Norma said. "I just think the public should know the truth about her."

After Norma finished her second mini muffin, a moist banana nut one, she returned to her room to pack up. She removed the Elvis-inspired bell-bottom pen and notepad from the motel desk, placed them on top of her belongings in her suitcase, and zipped the luggage up.

This trip had not been what she had imagined it would be. She wasn't returning home with Svetlana, and Liam was now dead.

But Norma was used to things not going her way.

She was a survivor.

She had survived her husband's death.

She had survived being a single parent.

She had survived Cookie abandoning her.

And now, like Queen Victoria, various presidents, and even the Pope, she had survived an assassination attempt.

NINETEEN

LIZ

Day Three
Monday, July 5, 2021

"He's dead?" I say.

"Yes," Jeff says. "It's breaking news. No details have been released yet about the cause of death. But I'm pretty sure there'll be speculation that Jennifer Addis had something to do with it."

"And, by extension, me too?" I ask.

"Unfortunately, it's a possibility," he says.

That's *not* what I wanted to hear.

"Where were you last night?" he asks.

"What do you mean?" I say.

"Were you with other people?" he says.

"Yeah, I was at work and went directly to my apartment after. I spent the night with my roommates."

"That's good," he says. "How about this morning?"

"At home with my roommates until I came here," I say.

"It's important to have alibis," he says.

"But I didn't do anything," I say.

"That's why you need them," he explains.

"Kevin Addis lives in New York, and I live in L.A. and work on *The Underdog*," I say. "Why would I need alibis?"

My phone makes a sound. A text from Doug: **On your way?**

I wonder if he's heard the news about Kevin Addis. If he has, I bet he's thrilled—even *better* ratings.

"That's my boss," I let Jeff know. "I have to pick up a few more contestants now."

"Be careful," he warns. "And remember to call the police right away to file a report about the extortion email. I'll also contact them to let them know I'm representing you. I'll need to be there if they want to question you again. I'm licensed in New York and L.A. and have contacts at both police departments."

"Okay," I say.

"I'll check in later," he says.

"Thanks for helping me."

He nods, stands up, and walks me to his office door.

"Don't worry, we'll get through this," he says.

I want to believe him, but I'm not so sure.

I'M RIDING in the town car to pick up the next group of contestants at the airport. I just got off with Detective Cooper in New York and reported the extortion email, which I forwarded to him. He had no updates for me about the loan payoff. I also gave him Jeff's information and let him know that he's now representing me.

The town car just pulled up in front of the airport terminal. I'm picking up three contestants who are competing against each other tomorrow night for a spot in the wildcard round. It's happening on elimination night when two existing contestants will be sent home from the show.

I look out the car window and see a bunch of paparazzi on the sidewalk, a common sight at LAX because of celebrities who fly in and out of this airport, especially during the summer when people go on vacation with their families. I wonder which celebrity they're here for today.

When I open the car door, a thousand bulbs flash in my eyes. That's when I realize the paparazzi are here for *me*. I step onto the curb, and they immediately swarm me, bombarding me with questions:

"Did you help The Singing Patient escape?"
"Where is Jennifer Addis?"
"How did Kevin Addis die?"

This is what Doug meant when he said *I'm* the show now.

I duck my head, hold onto my bag with both arms, and push through them until I get inside the airport. I hope they're not allowed there. I finally enter the terminal and quickly walk to the baggage carousel to meet the contestants, who are already there waiting for me.

Nolan, an Elvis-inspired swooner who filmed a TikTok of himself breaking into Graceland and singing *Unchained Melody* before being arrested, introduces himself.

"I'm Nolan," he says.

"I'm Liz," I say.

Sophie, an actress who served a couple of years in prison for her involvement in a multi-level marketing company, which was a front for a cult, chimes in.

"Sophie," she says, putting her hand out to shake mine.

"Nice to meet you," I say, shaking it back.

Angelique, a former Disney child star who went sailing with a man her father's age until he mysteriously disappeared while they were out at sea due to a supposed boating accident, looks me up and down. "Angelique," she cooly says while sucking on a vaping device.

"Come with me," I tell them.

They follow me to the airport exit. When we step out, the paparazzi are still there, camera ready, and snap dozens of pictures of us.

The wildcard trio couldn't be happier and pose for the cameras. Nolan takes a selfie with one of the paparazzi and quickly posts the picture across all of his social media platforms.

"Come on," I tell him, leading the trio to the town car.

We start to pile in when Angelique stops.

"Hip injury," she says. "From the boating accident. I need to sit shotgun."

"Fine," I say, even though I wanted to sit in the front with the driver.

Instead, I pile in the backseat next to Nolan, who is wedged between Sophie and me.

We pull away from the airport, heading to the studio for a soundcheck before tomorrow night's wildcard elimination night.

Nolan turns and asks me, "Did you do it?"

"What?" I say.

"Help Jennifer Addis escape so she could kill her husband?" he says.

All three of them turn their heads and look at me.

"No," I say. "I never met her until I picked her up."

"No judgment," he says. "We all gotta take care of ourselves. Late-stage capitalism, man."

"I didn't do it," I say.

"Can I get a picture with you to post?" he asks. "You're kinda famous now."

"Only if you ask your followers for tips about where Jennifer Addis might be," I say. "I need to find her. She's the only one who can clear my name."

"Deal," he says.

He takes a selfie of us in the backseat, posts it across his socials, and types underneath:

Anyone know where The Singing Patient is?

TWENTY

NORMA

Day Three
Monday, July 5, 2021

When Norma returned home from Los Angeles, she found the last person she expected to see on her doorstep—Cookie.

Cookie's eyes were red and puffy, and she immediately collapsed in Norma's arms.

"Liam's dead," she told Norma, weeping. "The police called. They found him in Los Angeles. He told me he was going there for business."

Some business, Norma thought.

"Oh my God," Norma said, feigning surprise.

"After losing Rose, I don't think I can survive this." Cookie wouldn't stop sobbing.

Norma held her daughter in her arms with a sturdy grasp. Cookie needed her now, and Norma, her mother, was the only person who could be there for her.

It reminded Norma of when Cookie was six and slipped while running to a swing set in the park. Norma remembered how Cookie had looked down in terror at her bloodied knees and then back up again at Norma for comfort and reassurance.

"Why don't you come in?" Norma told Cookie.

They pulled out of the embrace, and Norma unlocked the front door. She rolled her suitcase inside the house and turned on the lights. Everything in her home appeared untouched since she had left it a few days before.

"Where were you?" Cookie asked.

"I went to Albany to visit your grandparents' graves," Norma said. Cookie knew they were buried there. "I didn't make it for Mother's Day or Father's Day this year. The cemetery had a special ceremony on the Fourth of July, honoring fallen soldiers."

Cookie nodded and took a seat at the same wooden kitchen table where she had eaten all of her childhood meals.

"I'll be right back," Norma said. "I need to use the bathroom. I'll make us tea after."

Norma went to the bathroom, stood in front of the mirror above the sink, and reapplied the concealer on her neck to cover the bruises from Liam's fingerprints. She wasn't sure Cookie would even notice because she was very upset. But better safe than sorry.

NORMA AND COOKIE sipped on chamomile tea. Thankfully, Cookie had stopped crying.

"The police contacted me because I'm his emergency contact on his phone. They wanted me to fly to L.A. to identify him, but I told them I couldn't bear to do it. I gave them our dentist's phone number. They said they can identify him with his dental records," Cookie said.

"Did they mention how he died?" Norma asked.

"Murdered." Cookie choked on the word.

"Oh no," Norma said.

"The perpetrator stuck an ice pick in his eye. They think it caused a seizure that killed him."

That's why Liam had been convulsing and foaming at the mouth.

"I'm very sorry," Norma said.

"The police said there was no sign of forced entry into his room, which means whoever did it had a way in. They took his wallet too."

"Like a robbery gone bad?" Norma asked.

"They don't know yet," Cookie said.

"Maybe it was someone from the motel staff since they have room keys," Norma said.

Cookie paused.

"How did you know he was staying at a motel?" she asked Norma.

"I just assumed that after losing your home, you two were being frugal," Norma replied.

"How did you know that we lost our home?" Cookie said.

Norma's heart fluttered. Despite Cookie's bereaved state, she was still sharp as a tack.

"When I was volunteering at the hospital, I found out Rose died. After, I drove by your place to see how you were doing and saw the Zillow sign. I contacted the realtor, who told me you were selling because you were having trouble making your mortgage payments."

Cookie nodded her head. "I thought about asking you for money, but I didn't."

"I would've given it to you," Norma offered.

"Liam must've been terrified," Cookie said. "I wish I could've been there to protect him." She started crying again, and Norma got up from her chair to comfort her daughter again.

"You'll get through this," Norma told her.

"I don't think I can," Cookie said.

"You don't have a choice," Norma said.

TWENTY-ONE
LIZ

Day Three
Monday, July 5, 2021

I'm back at my apartment with my roommates after a long day at the studio doing a sound check for tomorrow night's wildcard elimination night.

Vince and Stefanie saw the pictures online the paparazzi snapped of me at LAX with the three new contestants. I'm stress-eating a tub of tart-flavored frozen yogurt with white chocolate chips while going through each of Nolan's social media accounts, scanning the comments underneath the picture he posted of us to see if there are any tips about where Jennifer Addis might be. I don't see anything.

My phone rings. It's Dad. "Hi," I say, picking up.

"Hi, sweetheart," he says. "You didn't call me this week for our weekly check-in, and I got worried."

"I'm sorry," I say. "I've had my hands full."

"So I've heard," he says. "The police called to ask if I knew about your student loans. I'm not exactly sure what's going on, but I told them I didn't. Because if I'd known, I would've helped you."

Shit. They called him.

"Did they mention the singer from the show who ran away?" I ask.

"Yeah. Something about her possibly paying off your loans so you'd look the other way," he says.

"I never met her before I picked her up," I say. "There's manipulated footage of me with her at the airport that may come out soon. I want you to know it's not real."

"I believe you, kid," he says.

I feel like crying out of guilt for bringing him into this mess. "Thanks," I say. "I'm sorry they called you."

"No need to be sorry. Next time, if you need help, please ask. After your Mom died, I didn't ask anyone for help because I was too proud. Don't be me," he says.

My eyes water, thinking about him losing the love of his life and how much he's done for me since. And I can't help but feel like the biggest disappointment ever.

"I love you," I say.

"Love you more," he says.

After we hang up, I turn to my roommates, who are glued to their phones, searching for any breaking news about Jennifer Addis.

"That was my Dad," I say. "The police contacted him."

"I can't find anything about where she might be or any details about Kevin Addis's death beyond the fact he died," Vince says.

"Me either," Stefanie says. "I've been checking different r/Underdog threads, and nothing."

"Maybe she went to try to find her daughter," Vince says. "Where is her daughter, anyway, now that her dad is dead?"

"Who knows," Stefanie says.

"What did the lawyer the DGA referred you to say?" Vince asks.

"He's taking my case on pro bono," I say. "He says he's going to help me."

I don't mention that under different circumstances, Jeff is the nice Jewish boy I think Mom hoped I'd end up with. Or that his comment about how the world needs more artists practically moved me to tears. Or that I felt my heart flutter when he walked me to his office door to say goodbye.

"That's nice of him," Stefanie says.

"Since he's not charging you, you should spend the money you would've spent on an attorney to hire a P.I. They'll be able to help you track down Jennifer Addis," Vince says.

"I can't afford to hire a P.I.," I say.

"I'm not sure you have a choice," he says, staring at his phone screen. His eyes pop out.

"What now?" I ask.

He turns his phone screen to face me. TMZ's website is pulled up. The lead story is the fake manipulated airport footage of me looking the other way as Jennifer Addis runs out of the United Terminal airport bathroom.

The extorters released it.

My phone makes a sound. It's a text from Jeff: **On it. Releasing a statement to the press right now.**

My phone makes another sound. Another text—this one from Doug: **My office. First thing tomorrow morning.**

Am I fired? I text back.

He doesn't respond.

TWENTY-TWO

NORMA

Day Four
Tuesday, July 6, 2021

Even though Cookie had abandoned her, Norma decided to be the bigger person in the relationship and not hold it against her.

Cookie was in bad shape, and Norma was her mother, so when Cookie asked if she could spend the night in her childhood bedroom, Norma let her. She even gave Cookie Oreo to sleep with for comfort, despite Cookie having abandoned him when she went to college and her having made fun of Norma for holding onto him.

It was morning now, and Norma was busy preparing breakfast for two. She had strategically placed a summer scarf around her neck. The bruising from Liam's fingers was still there. Norma hoped all traces of him would be gone in a few days time.

Cookie was on the phone with her job, explaining what had happened to Liam and that she needed time off. From what Norma gathered listening to Cookie's end, it sounded like they were sympathetic, probably because Cookie had lost both a baby and a fiancé in the same year.

Norma plated the French toast she had prepared on Cookie's favorite Hello Kitty plate and paired it with Cookie's first utensil set that was also Hello Kitty themed. Norma thought that seeing the pink fork with the cat's face and red bow on its tip and *Hello Kitty* painted in black cursive on its stem would cheer her daughter up. But she didn't want to eat.

"I have no appetite," Cookie told Norma. "Maybe I'll just take some coffee."

Norma bit her lip and decided to let it go. She wrapped the French toast in tinfoil and put it in the refrigerator for later.

When lunchtime rolled around, Cookie still didn't want to eat, even though Norma had prepared a grilled cheddar cheese sandwich with the crust cut off, sliced into triangles, just how Cookie liked it.

"I'm not hungry," Cookie said.

Norma ignored the comment and pulled out a yellow canister of Lipton ice tea powder from the cabinet. She unscrewed the blue lid, poured two heaping tablespoons of powder into two tall glasses, and stirred in some filtered water.

She took a sip of the tea. It was a little warm. She removed a large bag of ice from the freezer and dumped it into an ice bucket. The ice was in the shape of a block. She pulled out an ice pick from the utensil drawer and stabbed the block over and over again, breaking it into smaller pieces.

"Can you stop?" Cookie asked.

Norma looked up at her daughter, holding the ice pick. Cookie looked horrified.

"It's stuck together," Norma explained.

"Have you considered how using an ice pick right now might make me feel?" Cookie said.

"I'm sorry," Norma said, placing the pick in the sink.

"I'm not eating lunch," Cookie announced.

Norma had years of practice being resolute with her daughter, especially during her rebellious teenage years.

"You have to," Norma told Cookie firmly.

"But I feel nauseous," Cookie said. "Probably because I slept in a bedroom with a carpet that smells like urine. You really should have it cleaned."

Norma bristled. Cookie had *a lot* of nerve criticizing her and telling her what she needed to do when Norma opened her home to Cookie despite Cookie's mistreatment of her. Norma remembered the day she had relieved herself on Cookie's carpet and how it was the first thing that made her feel good in months after Cookie had abandoned her for the umpteenth time.

Now, Norma felt the urge to do it again. But she bit her tongue, willing herself to be the bigger person in their relationship yet again. Cookie's fiancé had just died, after all.

"Forget the grilled cheese sandwich," Norma said. "Let's go to the Cheesecake Factory for lunch and get some sunshine."

Cookie shrugged.

THE OUTDOOR MALL WAS BUSY. It was the week after the Fourth of July, and many people had taken it off.

Norma and Cookie sat in the outdoor seating section of The Cheesecake Factory, sharing a pepperoni pizza and Caesar salad that Norma had ordered for them to share.

Cookie was finally eating something, and Norma was glad to see it.

"Liam told me if anything ever happened to him, he wanted to be cremated," Cookie let Norma know.

Norma was relieved to hear this. The last thing she wanted to do was attend a burial service for the man who had almost killed her.

"That will probably be easier on you," Norma said.

"I've decided I don't want to get engaged again or try for another family," Cookie added.

While this was music to Norma's ears because Cookie and her would finally be back together, she knew she couldn't say the quiet part out loud.

"It's best not to make any decisions now," Norma said. "You've been through too much."

Cookie took a bite of the pepperoni pizza and chewed on it when a woman approached their table. At first, Norma didn't recognize her because Ruby, the actress, had transformed her long Julia Roberts auburn hair into a short blond bob.

Ruby walked right up to Cookie, almost breathless. "I've been waiting for this chance for over a year. After you moved, I had no way of contacting you to apologize."

"I think you're confused," Cookie told Ruby. "I don't know you."

"I was hired by—" Ruby said.

"You need to leave now," Norma interrupted her before Ruby could get another word out.

"No," Ruby dug in. "I spoke with my pastor about it, and even though I was struggling with money at the time, it's no excuse for what I did—"

"My daughter's fiancé was just murdered," Norma interrupted her again. "It's best you leave us alone."

"Oh my God," Ruby said. Her face went white, but she didn't move.

"If you don't go now, I'll call security," Norma warned her.

Ruby finally turned around and shuffled away.

"What was that about?" Cookie asked Norma.

"I don't know," Norma said. "Probably a mentally ill vagrant. They're everywhere these days."

"She didn't look homeless," Cookie said. She peeled a piece of pepperoni off her pizza slice, now distracted by her food. "Why did you get pepperoni?" she asked Norma.

"I thought you liked it," Norma said.

"Next time, get plain," Cookie said.

Norma was annoyed by Cookie's bossiness but let it go. She was focused on Ruby, watching her carefully. The actress kept walking into the distance, growing smaller and smaller until she finally disappeared.

TWENTY-THREE

LIZ

Day Four
Tuesday, July 6, 2021

"Everyone has seen the video of you looking the other way at the airport when Jennifer Addis fled," Doug tells me.

I'm in his office, sitting across from him. As usual, he has *Amadeus* playing on the television screen mounted on the wall behind him.

"The footage was manipulated," I say. "I never saw Jennifer Addis leaving that bathroom. Someone sent me that fake video, threatening to release it if I didn't pay them one hundred thousand dollars. It was an attempt to extort me. I filed a report with the police."

"I hear you," he says. "But perception is reality. And the studio can't employ a chaperone, which the public perceives as unable to safely deliver contestants to the show."

"Am I being fired now?" I ask.

"I'm doing my best to keep you here," he says. "But things are definitely more complicated now that Kevin Addis is dead. Everyone thinks Jennifer Addis is involved."

"And, by extension, me?" I ask.

He ignores my question. "Bottom line is you're now formally *on notice*," he says.

I'M at the Grove for wildcard elimination night, standing by the stage with the contestants about to perform.

When I first got here, Doug gave me the cold shoulder. I'm on very thin ice, even though I haven't done anything wrong.

"Can you take a picture of me?" Nolan asks me. He's dressed in full Elvis gear, black bell-bottom pants, and a gold leather jacket.

"Okay, I say.

He hands me his phone and poses in front of the red velvet rope.

"Make sure to get the stage behind me," he says.

"I am," I say and take a few pictures.

I return his phone, and he posts one of the pictures I took across all of his social media platforms.

"Are you ready for your first wildcard contestant?" C.J. calls out from the stage.

The audience applauds loudly.

"Nolan Jett, the stage is all yours!" C.J. shouts.

Nolan runs up the stairs. A screen behind him starts playing the footage that made him famous—his breaking into Graceland, followed by his arrest.

When the first few notes of *Jailhouse Rock* start, he pumps his fist in the air. A silver pole suddenly shoots out from the stage's ground, and he runs toward it. He twirls around it three times and picks up a prison baton prop from the corner of the stage. He thrusts his pelvis from side to side, holds the baton in the air, and motions for the audience to get up. Everyone stands up, dances, and sings with him until the last note—*Rock!*

The performance ends with a two-minute-long standing ovation. I scan *The Underdog's* social media accounts on my phone, monitoring the responses:

A STAR is born!

Will you be MY king???

There's your winner…

This will be a hard act to follow. But Sophie is called up and does just that. She sings *You Don't Own Me* with footage of her former cult in remote pastures, including their leader, who is now serving a twenty-year sentence, playing on the projector screen behind her. Sophie can barely hold back tears when she gets to the part about not being owned anymore and finally being free. After hitting her last note, she weeps alone on stage.

At first, the audience hesitates to applaud. But one member starts, and then everyone joins in a show of support. The social media comments are filled with praise and support:

SPEECHLESS RN

i'm gonna throw up this is so good

Straight to Broadway!

Angelique goes on next and sings an a cappella performance of *Mama Mia* with footage of the Titanic sinking from the movie behind her. She sings through her pain about being brokenhearted since her much older ex-boyfriend "mysteriously" disappeared on the yacht while she was with him. People online seem to love it as much as the audience:

Vicious and amazing.
I understand the song now.
Waiting for this cover on Spotify…

The show finally wraps. I walk to my car when my phone makes a sound. I take it out of my bag—a text from Jeff:

We need to talk, he texts.
What's going on? I text back.
There's more footage, he texts.
From the airport? I ask.
Footage connecting you to Kevin Addis's death.

TWENTY-FOUR

NORMA

Day Four
Tuesday, July 6, 2021

Norma was alone, curled up on the couch, watching TV.

Cookie had turned in early and was too upset to join her. She still had Oreo, and Norma didn't ask for him back because it seemed like Cookie needed him for comfort.

In the darkness of the night and the quiet of her house, Norma's worries began to fester. While she had gotten through the close call earlier in the day with Ruby, who had been ready to disclose to Cookie that Norma had hired her to take fake staged adulterous pictures with Liam, Norma had much bigger fears to agonize about.

Would the police investigation into Liam's death uncover that she was the one who stuck the ice pick in his eye? She had done everything possible to destroy any traces of her DNA. And thank God there were no cameras in the motel's hallways. Still, there was always a chance a tiny fragment of her DNA might've been left behind. And what if someone had heard them who she was unaware of?

Norma tried to reassure herself that if the police did somehow end up connecting her to Liam's death, she could always explain the truth. She had done it in self-defense because he had tried to murder her. She had aimed for his eye instead of his neck because she never wanted to kill him. The only problem with that story was she had taken his wallet and fled.

Norma was also worried about what Liam had told her before he died. The hospital knew Rose and Sadie had been switched at birth and had opened an investigation to find out how it had happened.

Even though, according to Liam, Cookie didn't yet know that Rose was alive, Norma knew it was only a matter of time before she found out the truth. If the hospital had been in touch with Liam because Sadie's parents had discovered he was her father through Ancestry.com, they would soon reach out to Cookie, who was Rose's Mom, especially since he was now dead.

Norma tried comforting herself that while Cookie knew Norma had been volunteering there when Rose was born, she would never accuse her own mother of switching Rose with a dead infant the way Liam had.

Norma shoved the bad thoughts out of her mind and channel-surfed. Thank God for television. *Dateline* was on, but she didn't want to be reminded of murder. She kept flipping stations until she came across *The Underdog.*

It was wildcard and elimination night. Three new performers, including a young Elvis wannabe swooner, would have the chance to secure a wildcard spot, and two of the show's original contestants would be cut.

Norma watched the show until the end, hoping Svetlana would get the boot. Unfortunately, she didn't. The

Singing Patient got the most votes, and wretched Svetlana came in second.

At least I have my Cookie back, Norma thought.

That's what mattered most. She just had to make sure it stayed that way.

At the show's end, *The Underdog* host stood on the stage with all the contestants. "We want to congratulate everyone that made it through to next week's show and bid farewell to those who are parting ways with us tonight," he said. The audience members applauded, and the contestants hugged each other.

"We now have a special request from you, the viewers," he continued. "Like too many Americans impacted by senseless violent crime, *The Underdog* family tragically has been too. Kevin Addis, the husband of Jennifer Addis, who you all know as The Singing Patient, was killed. The police are asking for your help to find the perpetrator."

Norma had heard about The Singing Patient escaping a mental hospital. She wondered if the woman had killed her husband after fleeing. The show would probably never admit that because The Singing Patient was clearly good for ratings. She had gotten the most votes tonight.

"Here's a picture of Kevin Addis," the host continued. "If you have any information connected to his death, please call 1-888-KEV-ADDI."

Norma's television screen filled with a picture of the man's face. She stared at it in disbelief.

He wasn't The Singing Patient's husband.

It was *Liam.*

r/TheUnderdog
Posted by Calming4ce_
The Singing Patient!!!

HUSBAND K!LLED

Steffed_up
the police just announced it was with an *ice pick*

Justin-Case97
i guess the singing patients not gonna win

Calming4ce_
Maybe they'll film her in prison.

Steffed_up
what if it wasn't her?

Calming4ce_
It had to be. Her husband committed her, and she wanted
revenge.

Justin-Case97
no wonder he didn't want her doing the show, he prob knew she
was gonna kill him once she got out

Calming4ce_
Have you heard about r/SingingPatientFanFic?

Steffed_up
what's that?

Calming4ce_

A place to write the singing patient's origin story.

Steffed_up

like fan fiction?

Calming4ce_

I think so. My coworker told me about it.

Justin-Case97

im gonna check it out

TWENTY-FIVE

NORMA

Day Four
Tuesday, July 6, 2021

Norma couldn't stop staring at the television screen. Her mouth hung open in shock.

The Singing Patient's husband was Liam?

How could that be?

Cookie mentioned the police had contacted her because she was Liam's emergency contact. And Norma had his wallet.

Did the police discover another phone or a different wallet after they had contacted Cookie? They had to have somehow connected him to The Singing Patient.

Norma got up from the couch, went to her bedroom, and pulled out Liam's wallet from underneath her mattress. She hadn't looked at the contents inside after she had stolen it. Norma had planned to buy a shredder later in the week to turn everything inside into dust. She took out his driver's license and credit cards and studied them. They all had Liam's name.

The police had to have other items that tied him to this other identity. They wouldn't have made a public plea on *The Underdog* if they didn't.

Was Liam leading a double life?

It was only a matter of time before they contacted Cookie to let her know if she didn't find out sooner on her own. *The Underdog* was a very popular show, and the hunt for The Singing Patient's husband would make national news if it hadn't already.

Norma now feared for herself in a way she hadn't before. Even though she had tried to destroy all traceable DNA, Liam wasn't a random man killed in an Elvis-inspired motel. He was the husband of the most sought-after woman in America, a fugitive who had escaped a psychiatric hospital and sang like Cher.

The media coverage surrounding the investigation into his death would be twenty-four-seven. The police would do everything possible to find the perpetrator because it was such a high-profile case.

Norma stuffed Liam's wallet back underneath her mattress and went to her kitchen. She removed a wine glass from the cabinet and a bottle of Pinot Grigio from the refrigerator. She poured herself a glass and drank it in one swoop. She then poured herself another and returned to the living room with it.

Norma sat on the couch and turned the channel from *The Underdog* to a cable news station. The news coverage was all about Kevin Addis's death. How someone had killed him in a grizzly murder with an ice pick.

They played a video of his wife, The Singing Patient, fleeing the airport and *The Underdog's* hired chaperone looking the other way. After, the pundits speculated whether Jennifer Addis killed her husband. They also wondered if the show's chaperone, whose student loans had likely been paid off to look the other way while she fled, might've been in on his murder too.

Norma took another sip of Pinot Grigio. If she stepped back and looked at this picture from the perspective of an uninvolved observer, it seemed the media was running with a specific narrative—one that didn't involve her at all.

This was *good* news for Norma.

She felt the tightening in her chest soften and let out a sigh of relief.

Her life had been very hard. But maybe, finally, for once, God had decided to throw her a bone.

Day Four
Tuesday, July 6, 2021

Everyone left, including the contestants, who caught a shuttle back to the hotel they're staying at. The shopping center's employees are pulling the makeshift stage apart.

I'm waiting for Jeff, who texted me that he's on his way here to discuss the new footage connecting me to Kevin Addis's death. He said it couldn't wait and that he preferred to speak in person. I'm really worried and have no idea what footage he's talking about that could possibly connect me to Kevin Addis's murder.

I scroll through my phone to see if there's anything online about it. I read the breaking news that someone killed Kevin Addis with an ice pick the same night as Jennifer Addis sent in her taped surprise performance. Social media is drowning in rumors that she did it. I notice in some online corners there's chatter that I helped her, just like I supposedly helped her flee from the airport. I'm deep into scrolling on my phone when Svetlana walks up to me and interrupts me.

"Hi," she says.

"Did you miss the shuttle?" I ask her.

"I'm catching an Uber instead," she says.

"Do you need me to call security to wait with you?" I say.

"It's okay," she says. "Thanks for helping me a couple of nights ago. I haven't seen that crazy fan since then."

"No problem. It's my job," I say.

"You could've pretended to look the other way, especially since I was an asshole to you when you picked me up at the airport," she says.

She has a point, but whatever.

"I've moved on," I let her know.

"I feel bad about threatening you and your job. Someone told me you were living out of your car before you started working for *The Underdog*," she said.

Doug must've told someone that he found me sleeping in my car on the day of my interview, and word got out.

"It's fine," I say.

"I know you're in deep shit now because of the Jennifer Addis situation, and I want to help you," she says.

Why the change of heart?

I can't help but wonder if she has an ulterior motive. Her own angle. I'm just not sure what it is.

"I don't think you can help me," I say. "Jennifer Addis is the only one who can clear my name, and I have no idea where she is."

"That's what I wanted to talk to you about," she says. "Can I show you something?"

"Okay," I say.

She pulls out her phone and plays Jennifer's surprise

performance from a couple of days ago. The a cappella cover of *I Won't Back Down* by Tom Petty. It's uploaded on YouTube now and has been played over seven million times.

"I already watched it," I let Svetlana know.

"Did you notice the lamp above her?" she asks, pointing to her phone screen.

"I hadn't really. It looks like a basic dark lampshade," I say. "The kind Home Depot sells for twenty bucks."

Svetlana screenshots the image and zooms in on it. Up close, more details come into focus. It's a dark green stained glass lampshade. "I know it's hard to see since the shade is overdue for a cleaning, but do you see that?" she asks, zooming in further.

I notice a long piece of lighter green stained glass embedded in the darker green glass. And there are two tiny orange dots at the end of it, right at the rim of the shade.

"That's a dragonfly," Svetlana says.

"Now that you pointed it out, I see it," I say.

"This lampshade is one of the rarest Tiffany's hanging head shades ever made. It's a dragonfly chandelier circa the early nineteen hundreds. Christie's has sold only a few at auction over the last century for many millions. I have contacts who can track down who purchased them. It might give you a clue of where she filmed her performance and where she might be now."

"Really?" I say.

Svetlana nods her head.

I still don't understand why she suddenly wants to help me. Yes, I helped her with the obsessed fan, but it wasn't that big of a deal. And she was so hostile when we first met. I don't know if I can trust her.

"Why are you doing this?" I ask her.

"I lived out of my car too before," she admits. "Wouldn't wish it on anyone."

I nod my head. "Me either," I say.

"We all gotta do what we need to do to survive," she says.

"Hi," Jeff calls out. He's approaching us.

"Is that your boyfriend?" she asks.

"Lawyer," I say.

"Let me get your number," she says. She hands me her phone to put my number in her contacts, and I type my cell phone number.

"I'll be in touch if I hear anything," she says. "Again, I'm sorry about before."

"It's okay," I say.

She walks away as Jeff comes up to me, looking very worried. Before I have the chance to tell him about the lampshade, he says, "I heard from my contact at the LAPD that Kevin Addis was killed in a motel near here."

"Near The Grove?" I ask.

"Yes," he says. "It's called The Heartbreak Motel. There's speculation he flew out here to speak to the producers about Jennifer Addis's disappearance."

"My boss, Doug, never mentioned anything about him coming," I say.

"There's a video of you blowing through a red light near the motel right after he was murdered," Jeff says.

"Two nights ago, I went through a red light after leaving here. I had just seen Jennifer Addis's surprise performance and was shook by it," I say. "But I've never heard of that motel or ever been there. I went right home after finishing up here like I always do."

"I believe you," he says. "But you'll need some evidence to back up your claim."

It feels like I can't catch a break. Like all the stars are aligned against me. I was worried about getting a moving violation and my insurance premiums going up when I went through the red light. Now, I have much bigger things to worry about. Tears swell in my eyes, and I really don't want to cry in front of Jeff.

"Thanks for coming," I say. "I don't want to make a scene in front of you. I better go home."

He moves in to hug me. I'm unsure if this is allowed in an attorney relationship since I've never hired one. But I let him, and I don't want to let go.

r/TheSingingPatientFanFic

Posted by Calming4ce_

Origin Story

Is anyone here?

Steffed_up

i am.

Calming4ce_

Maybe we could try coming up with her story?

Justin-Case97

im bad at art

Steffed_up

my high school english teacher told me i was a talented writer.

Calming4ce_

Wow us.

Steffed_up

promise not to judge?

Justin-Case97

waiting…

Steffed_up

 Jennifer heard the front door slam shut. She sat up in bed and stared down at her stuffed stomach. Eight months pregnant and alone.

 She teared up, remembering the joy she had felt when she

first learned she was going to have a baby girl. A bittersweet moment, knowing her own mother would never meet her granddaughter since she had died when Jennifer was a young girl.

Jennifer was an only child, and her ailing father lived in another state. Her husband was her only family, but he was never there.

Jennifer reached for the antidepressant pills on her nightstand. It was the first time in her life she had taken them. The psychiatrist had told her depression was common in pregnancy due to hormonal fluctuations.

But maybe it wasn't the hormones. Maybe it was that she was on bed rest, and her husband, who she needed the most, was always gone.

Thoughts?

Justin-Case97

only got through the first paragraph, adhd, I think it's too long

Calming4ce_

It might be better if you started when she goes crazy. Grab us from the start.

Miz_Beleaf

New here. Okay if I try?

Justin-Case97

fine w me

Calming4ce_

Go ahead.

Miz_Beleaf

When we returned from the hospital, I set up a baby monitor

in the nursery. Friends had warned me that I wouldn't get much sleep.

But during our first night back home, my baby girl never woke up. I put her in her crib at 7 p.m. and went to bed, exhausted from my delivery and hospital stay.

I woke up at 5 a.m. and realized the monitor had never made a sound.

Or maybe it had, and we'd slept through it.

I panicked, fearing she had needed me and I hadn't been there for her.

I ran to the nursery and put my hand on her chest to make sure she was breathing. Thankfully, her heart was beating strongly, and she was sleeping peacefully.

The following night, when she slept through the night again, I started to worry. It didn't seem normal. What if something was wrong with her? I called the pediatrician, who told me to enjoy it while it lasted because her sleeping patterns would inevitably change.

Later, when I woke her to feed her, she made a strange sound—almost like a growl. *Had I imagined it?* My doctor had educated me about postpartum depression and psychosis.

But that night, when I changed her diaper before putting her down, I heard it again. This time, there was no mistaking it. It was a loud, animal-like growl.

I was scared but still had to change her. I didn't want her to get a diaper rash. I put her on the changing table to remove the dirty diaper, lifting each wing, when she swiped my palm with her tiny hand.

I'd heard baby nails were sharp, and hers were no exception. A drop of blood bubbled on my pointer finger and dropped on her stomach.

That's when I noticed it—the *black fur* above her belly button.

Justin-Case97

still too long

Calming4ce_

It reminded me of a short story I read in college about a woman who turned into a wolf. Are you trying to get a book deal from this?

Miz_Beleaf

Not necessarily.

Calming4ce_

Then I guess it doesn't matter.

Steffed_up

don't listen to them! it's great.

Calming4ce_

One small thing: I think it would be more impactful to use the husband's name, Kevin, and the daughter's name if you can find it online.

Miz_Beleaf

Okay.

Steffed_up

can't wait to read more!

Miz_Beleaf

Thanks.

TWENTY-SEVEN

NORMA

Day Five
Wednesday, July 7, 2021

Norma woke up early and called Little Saint Mary's to see if her former volunteer job was still there for her, as Jay had promised a year ago.

She needed to find out more about the investigation they had launched into Rose and Sadie being switched. And being at the hospital was the best way to find out where it stood. When Jay told her to come by, she was relieved.

After she hung up, Cookie woke up and stumbled to the kitchen table for breakfast. Norma plated a slice of home-made banana bread she had frozen and unthawed on Cookie's Hello Kitty plate and poured her a glass of milk in the matching Hello Kitty cup.

Cookie still didn't have much of an appetite and only picked at the slice of banana bread.

Norma knew what she was about to tell her daughter

was going to be another blow, but she decided it was best if Cookie heard the news about Liam from her.

"Liam was married," Norma announced.

"What?" Cookie said.

"It's all over the news," Norma said.

"What are you talking about?" Cookie asked.

"He was The Singing Patient's husband," Norma explained.

Cookie looked confused. "The woman who ran away from the hospital?"

Norma nodded her head. "He must have been leading a double life," Norma continued.

"I don't believe you," Cookie said.

"It's true," Norma said.

"Is this some kind of intervention to snap me out of my grief?" Cookie asked.

"No," Norma said.

Cookie took out her phone and started scrolling. "Oh my God," she said.

"I'm sorry," Norma said.

Norma wasn't sorry at all.

Liam was a bad man. She was glad he was dead as long as his death was blamed on someone else.

"Did you ever suspect anything?" Norma asked.

Cookie shook her head, still scrolling her phone in shock. "I mean, he went to the gym a lot..."

Norma nodded her head. "Sorry you had to find out this way."

Cookie suddenly shrieked and threw her phone on the ground, cracking the screen.

Norma was surprised by the outburst of emotion, though it was understandable.

"FUCK HIM!" Cookie yelled. "They were married and had a baby four months ago!"

"I can't imagine how that must feel," Norma said.

"No, you can't," Cookie said.

Why did Cookie have to be so mean even when Norma was trying to be understanding?

"I've been devastated ever since I found out he was killed," Cookie said. "But now I just feel angry. Rage. It's an unimaginable betrayal."

Norma thought about how uncomplicated her daughter was. Cookie had stapled herself to Liam, the first man who had given her a crumb of attention. Run toward him like a Labradoodle chasing after a piece of bologna. It was inevitable that something like this would happen.

"Do you still want to be responsible for his body?" Norma asked her.

"Who knows if I'll even be allowed to make arrangements for it now since he was married to someone else. But, no. Fuck no. And fuck him. And as sad as I am that Rose died..." Cookie struggled to get the words out. "I'm glad she never had to find out the truth about her father."

Norma had forgotten about Rose for a minute. What would happen when Cookie learned she was still alive? Maybe Cookie would decide she didn't want any memories of Liam and let Rose be raised by the other couple, who Liam had said were gearing up for a legal fight to keep her.

Cookie stood up from the kitchen table. "I'm calling my job," she announced. "I'm going back to work. I don't want to spend another second of my life thinking about that dirtbag."

"That's my girl," Norma said.

TWENTY-EIGHT

LIZ

Day Five
Wednesday, July 7, 2021

I'm sitting in Doug's office. There's an older woman with red dyed hair sitting beside him, whom I've never met before.

"This is Gene from H.R.," Doug says, motioning to her.

"The studio has specific policies," she says. "They can't employ someone who may be implicated in the murder of a contestant's family member."

I turn to Doug. "You think I'm involved with Kevin Addis's death?"

"Murder," he corrects me. "I don't know what to think. There's footage of you blowing through a red light near the motel where he was killed."

"I was at work the night he died when Jennifer Addis sent in her surprise performance. You were with me. Yes, I went through a red light because I was distracted after watching it. But I went directly home. Back to my apartment and spent the entire night with my roommates. They can tell you. I'm not a murderer. I can't even kill a spider."

"This isn't personal," Gene says. "It's protocol."

I want to scream at her that it is *deeply* personal. Because I only have one month of rent saved. And once that's gone, I'll be back in my car on the street unless I break Dad's heart again and ask him for help.

But it's worse than that. Once I'm fired, everyone will assume the studio let me go because I'm connected to Kevin Addis's death. The truth is everyone probably already thinks I am. I'll never be able to get a job again in Holly- wood or elsewhere.

"We're offering you two weeks severance, which will be included in your final paycheck if you sign this paperwork," Gene says. "You can apply for Cobra after this month's health insurance runs out."

She tries to hand me a piece of paper and a pen to sign it, but I don't take either from her.

How can they do this to me when I haven't done anything wrong?

I need to speak with Jeff. He mentioned I shouldn't speak to the police again without him there. I probably shouldn't be talking to Gene and Doug without him here, either.

"I'm not signing anything," I say. "My attorney will be in touch with you."

I stand up and leave.

TWENTY-NINE

NORMA

Day Five
Wednesday, July 7, 2021

Norma arrived at Little Saint Mary's with a summer scarf draped around her neck and a thick coat of coral lipstick. Jay greeted her and swiftly brought her into the room where he had guided her volunteer training session over a year before.

They sat down on the same maroon-colored cushioned chairs, and he smiled at her with his California white teeth like no time had passed at all. "Nice to see you again," he said.

"Likewise," Norma said.

"The hospital was planning to reach out to you, anyway. It was serendipitous that you called," he said.

"Oh?" Norma said.

"I know you left under the worst circumstances due to your granddaughter," he said. "There's currently an investigation underway related to what happened."

"What do you mean?" Norma asked.

"A medical error occurred," Jay said. "I can't say much more than that."

"Are you suggesting Rose didn't die of SIDS?"

"Again, I really can't get into any details," Jay insisted.

"Is the hospital the one responsible for her death?" Norma pressed.

"An investigator is coming in now to speak with you. She'll explain everything." He quickly stood up and left.

Norma started to feel a sense of agita.

A woman with blunted brown bangs entered the room carrying a laptop. "Cecile Strong," she said. Cecile put out her hand and gave Norma a no-nonsense handshake.

"Hello," Norma said, limply shaking it back.

Cecile sat across from Norma and looked her directly in the eyes. "I've been hired to investigate a medical error that occurred on July 5, 2020, related to your granddaughter Rose Butterfly Case."

Norma bristled at hearing Rose's middle name again.

Cookie and that awful, lying, cheating imposter of a man had named Rose after Liam's dead birth mother instead of Norma, and they hadn't even chosen "Norma" as her middle name. It still made Norma burn inside.

"Is there anything you want to tell me?" Cecile asked Norma.

"About what?" Norma said.

"According to various hospital personnel testimonies, the day Rose died when you called for help, you didn't mention to anyone that she was your granddaughter until later that day."

"I tried performing CPR on my granddaughter. When it didn't work, I screamed for help. A bunch of doctors and nurses rushed in to try to save her. Would yelling in that moment that she was my granddaughter have helped them or changed the outcome?" Norma said, choked up.

Cecile nodded her head, unconvinced by Norma's display of emotion.

"After you left that day, you never returned to the hospital," Cecile said.

"Would you want to return to the place where your granddaughter died?" Norma pretended to hold back tears.

"You're here now…" Cecile said, letting the sentence hang in the air.

"I was bereft," Norma said. "I needed to get away from here. The past year has been one of the worst years of my life."

Norma finally admitted something truthful. It had been one of the worst years of her life due to being estranged from Cookie. Maybe the most horrible year of all. Even worse than the year after Ray died.

"So why are you back here now?" Cecile asked Norma.

"I finally realized the only way I can heal is by being around other babies," Norma lied.

"I'm sorry to inform you that you're not going to be allowed to volunteer at Little Saint Mary's due to our investigation," Cecile said.

"What are you suggesting?" Norma said. "You think I had something to do with my granddaughter's death?" Norma put her hand on her heart, aghast. She could put on a show, especially when a camera was rolling, and she had noticed one in the corner of the room when she first walked in.

"Your granddaughter is alive," Cecile announced.

"What?" Norma said. Her mouth hung open in shock.

"Rose was switched with another baby girl, Sadie Romano, who died. Sadie's parents, Brooke and Anthony

Romano, mistakenly took Rose home, thinking she was theirs. But it turns out Rose has a rare genetic disorder. When they went on Ancestry.com to find out if they had any relatives with it, they discovered they weren't her biological parents and that your son-in-law is, who is also registered on the site. They contacted the hospital, who informed them that he also had a baby girl born here the same day as Sadie. Someone switched Sadie and Rose."

Cecile didn't know Liam wasn't Norma's son-in-law. And it didn't sound like she knew he was dead, either.

"You're saying Rose is alive?" Norma asked.

"Yes," Cecile said.

"Are you sure?" Norma said.

"Yes," Cecile said again.

"You mentioned she has a rare genetic disorder—is she okay?" Norma asked.

Cecile nodded her head.

"Can I see her?" Norma said.

"I'm not sure about that," Cecile said. "The Romanos are gearing up for a legal fight to keep her, and you're currently involved in an investigation to determine who switched the two girls."

"The hospital thinks I switched my granddaughter with a dead baby?" Norma asked.

"I didn't say that," Cecile said. "I said we're in the process of an investigation to determine who removed Sadie's identification bracelets and put them on Rose."

"How could anyone do that?" Norma asked, confused. "Those bracelets are put on very tightly."

"Sadie's were loosened because her mother had informed her delivery team that there was a family history of a circulation disorder," Cecile said.

"Maybe you should be investigating the doctors and nurses," Norma fired back.

"We have a list of everyone who was working at the hospital that day and are going through it methodically," Cecile said.

"Aren't there cameras? I see one in here," Norma said, pointing to the one on the ceiling in the corner of the room. "Can't you tell who did it that way?"

"The cameras weren't working that day due to a malware attack that targeted multiple hospitals in the area," Cecile responded.

"This doesn't sound like a very well-run hospital, and because of it, I've been deprived of seeing my granddaughter for an entire year." Norma let out a small sob. "I'm going to seek legal counsel. It's slanderous to imply I could've been involved in this depraved scandal."

"Our attorney contacted your daughter a couple of days ago to let her know," Cecile said. "We're waiting to hear back about how she plans to proceed. We assume your son-in-law already told her after finding out. Legally, the hospital also has to notify her, but she hasn't gotten back to us yet."

Cookie never mentioned the call. But Norma hadn't seen Cookie on her phone much since Liam died, apart from calling her job after she found out about his double life. She had been likely ignoring calls during the ordeal.

"After your son-in-law found out, he came here threatening people and needed to be escorted out by our security team. We hope your daughter will be more cooperative," Cecile added.

That sounded like Liam.

"Liam was never my son-in-law," Norma clarified. "My

daughter and him were engaged. And he was killed a couple of days ago in Los Angeles."

"What?" Cecile said, trying to mask her surprise.

"He's dead," Norma said. "It turns out he was living a double life. He was married to The Singing Patient."

"The woman who fled the psychiatric hospital?" Cecile asked.

"Yes," Norma said. "My daughter just found out."

"I see," Cecile said. She typed something on her laptop's keyboard.

"Maybe he was the one who switched Rose and Sadie," Norma said. "I saw him in the nursery the day Rose was born. Maybe he wanted to make her disappear because he was married to someone else. Maybe he came here making a big scene like he cared about what had happened to make himself look innocent."

Cecile nodded her head, mulling over Norma's hypothesis.

"All I know is that I've lost an entire year with my granddaughter. One I'll never get back," Norma said. She began to cry loudly.

Cecile pulled a Kleenex from the box on the small side table and offered it to Norma. Norma took it and blew her nose.

Origin Story

Here is **Part Two**, thanks to Steff's encouragement. I used the husband's and daughter's names because of Calming4ce suggestion.

Kevin came home from work late like he'd done almost every day during the last trimester of my pregnancy. The first thing I did was show him the black hairy spot on Juliet's stomach. It looked like someone had pasted a small patch of animal fur above her belly button.

"Look," I said, pointing to it.

"Weird," he said casually. "Did you call the doctor?"

"She was out of the office today," I said. "They said she'd reach out to me tomorrow."

"Okay," he said.

"She also scratched me," I said, showing Kevin the small cut on my pointer finger.

"Everyone warned us about baby claws," he said. "Looks like a little paper cut. You'll probably live, but I'll take over tonight. Sounds like you could use a break."

That night, I had trouble falling asleep. I realized a sense of unease was taking hold.

When I woke up the following morning, Kevin was downstairs feeding Juliet with a bottle of breastmilk I had pumped the day before.

"Everything okay?" I asked.

"Perfect," he said, smiling as he lifted her in the air. She seemed happy and content with him, unlike with me.

"Gotta get to work," he said. "I have a client dinner tonight."

"Again?" I asked.

"A big one," he said. As soon as he handed Juliet to me, she growled again.

"Did you hear that?" I asked him.

"Nope," he said. He was busy rinsing his breakfast cereal bowl with water in the kitchen sink before putting it in the dishwasher.

"She growled at me," I said.

He looked at me strangely.

"Maybe get out of the house today," he said. "You could use the air."

I nodded, ate a bite of yogurt, and swallowed a few vitamins and my antidepressant.

After he left, I put Juliet back in her crib for a morning nap.

Her pediatrician returned my call about the black hair on her stomach and explained that it could be poliosis. She told me to bring her in if any other patches came up because they could be a sign of autoimmune issues like a thyroid disorder.

I hung up and went to the bathroom to take a shower. I felt the need to lock the door behind me.

Was I scared of my baby girl?

I quickly showered, got out, and dried myself off when I heard a *howl*. I ran from the bathroom to the crib.

Juliet was on all fours, howling to an imaginary moon. I immediately FaceTimed Kevin to show him, but he, of course, didn't pick up. I took a video of her and sent it to him.

I frantically opened all the shades and windows in the nursery, scared of what might come next. A neighbor in the house next door to us waved to me from their deck. I waved back, wondering if I should invite her over because I didn't want to be alone.

I turned back around to look at Juliet, and she was fine—acting like a normal baby again in her crib.

I quickly gathered my things, picked her up, put her in her stroller, and walked to our local park. I sat down on a bench and positioned her stroller next to me.

As the hours passed, she stayed asleep the entire time. I kept texting Kevin to ask if he had seen the video I had sent him, but he didn't respond.

At one point, an elderly woman walked by us and said, "You're so lucky." I smiled tightly back at her.

I was growing more and more anxious about returning home alone with Juliet. A pit of dread formed in my stomach. Things did not feel all right.

It was almost dark. I was hungry and tired from sitting alone on a park bench all day. I willed myself to go home.

When we got back to the house, I texted Kevin again, who finally responded. He said he never got the video I had sent him and said he'd see me around eleven.

I checked our text thread. The video wasn't there. I scanned the photos on my phone, searching for it there too.

It had disappeared.

Justin-Case97

was the video deleted or did she never record and send it?

Calming4ce_

I think she's purposefully leaving it open to interpretation.

Justin-Case97

im into this now fyi

Steffed_up

You're a great writer. Please keep going!

Miz_Beleaf

Thx. Busy now, will try to post part three soon.

THIRTY

LIZ

Day Five
Wednesday, July 7, 2021

I'm speaking to Jeff on the phone, pacing in my living room around the couch. My roommates are seated, scrolling on their phones.

"I was fired," I tell him. "They think I'm involved with Kevin Addis's murder because of the footage of me going through the red light near his motel. H.R. tried to get me to sign severance paperwork, but I didn't. I thought I should speak with you first."

"Glad you didn't sign it," he says. "No charges have been brought against you. They let you go on a no-basis. I'll be in touch with them."

My other line rings. It's Dad.

"My Dad's calling me," I let Jeff know. "I need to take it."

"Let's plan to check in later," Jeff says.

"Okay," I say. "Thanks again for your help."

"You got it," he says. "Talk soon."

"Bye," I say before picking up the other line. "Hi, Dad. How are you?"

"How are YOU?" he asks. "I've been watching the news about the singer's husband's murder. Maybe you should come home and lay low with your old man."

While it's tempting to run back to my childhood home and stay with him now, that won't solve any of my problems. There's still only one way for me to get out of this mess: finding Jennifer Addis, who can explain that I had nothing to do with her disappearance.

"I really appreciate the offer, but I can't go back to Chicago right now."

"If you change your mind, I'm here," he says.

"Thanks. I love you," I say.

"Love you more," he says.

After we hang up, I turn to my roommates.

"About that P.I.," Vince says. "It's way past time to hire one."

"What now?" I say.

He shows me his phone. TMZ's website is pulled up again. And their lead story is about me. More footage—me blowing through the red light near the Heartbreak Motel.

"That motel is right next to the Grove. I went through the red light on my way home from work because I was distracted after watching Jennifer Addis's surprise performance. I had no idea Kevin Addis was in L.A., and I've never been to that motel."

"This situation will only get worse until Jennifer Addis clears you," Vince says. "You need outside help to find her. I spoke with my friend. He recommended a local P.I. firm called L.A. Intelligence."

"I already told you I can't afford to hire a private investigator," I say. "It costs too much."

"I wish I had the money to lend you," Stefanie says.

"Same," Vince says. "But I can barely afford my student loan payments each month."

"Maybe you should charge it on your credit card," Stefanie says.

"You should," Vince says. "You're out of options now."

"Maybe not," I say. "I have enough for a plane ticket to New York."

"What will you do there?" Stephanie asks me.

"I can go back to the hospital. Maybe Jennifer told someone there where she planned to go," I say.

"But she doesn't speak. She only sings," Vince says. "How could she have told anyone anything?"

"Maybe she did speak to someone, and we don't know about it," I say. "I have a cousin who lives in Manhattan that I can probably stay with."

"You shouldn't do anything without letting your attorney know first," Vince says.

I doubt Jeff would approve of me playing detective, but I have no other choice. I'll tell him after I land.

I start packing.

THIRTY-ONE
NORMA

Day Five
Wednesday, July 7, 2021

Norma left the hospital, feeling good about her talk with the investigator. Of course, she had never wanted to kill Liam. But it sure was convenient to have him dead and be able to blame him for the baby switcheroo.

He was the perfect suspect. He was not only there, but he had a motive for wanting to get rid of Rose. He was leading a double life and had another family.

What possible motive could the investigators dig up for poor old Grandma Norma? None.

Norma decided to swing by the grocery store on her way home to pick up some of Cookie's favorites: apple sauce squeezes, cheddar goldfishies, Dino-shaped chicken nuggets, and a bottle of Cookie's favorite celebratory drink—Martinelli's sparkling apple cider.

Norma thought back fondly on all of the times they had shared a bottle of Martinelli's together at the kitchen table.

After Cookie won the spelling bee in 1st grade, the Pi contest in 3rd grade, and The Girl Scout Gold Award.

The apple hadn't fallen far from the tree. Cookie, like Norma, had always been one smart *Cookie*.

Norma felt a skip in her step as she walked through grocery aisles.

Things were finally looking up.

It had been a long time coming.

NORMA WAS DRIVING HOME from the market, listening to the car radio, when *Rise Up* came on. It was the original version. Norma begrudgingly had to admit that she thought Svetlana's cover on *The Underdog* had been better, even if Svetlana was a terrible person.

As Norma drove, she took in the song's lyrics for the first time and was astounded. It was as if someone had written the song for her.

She, too, had been underestimated, cast away, and almost left for dead. Yet she kept rising despite the staggering headwinds life had thrown her way.

She turned up the volume on her car stereo and sang *Rise Up* as loudly as she could. Her cheeks flushed cherry red. Tears flowed out of her like a natural spring waterfall.

She was the phoenix rising from the ashes. The orange sun emerging after a category five hurricane. She was Jesus Christ resurrected on the cross.

No one could stop her.

Norma smiled proudly through her tears and pulled up to her house when she saw a police car parked in front.

Posted by Miz_Beleaf

Origin Story

Part Three:

It had been two months since I had brought Juliet home, and my mental health had deteriorated. I met with my psychiatrist, who prescribed two new different antidepressants.

I asked Kevin to pick them up, which was all he did to help me. He was always gone, busy courting a new client or placating an existing one.

The new medications made me feel worse.

The nights were the hardest. The pediatrician had been right. Juliet's sleeping habits quickly changed. She developed colic and cried all night long.

One night, I was alone and had reached the end of my rope. I had tried everything to soothe her: bouncing her on my knees, feeding her, and singing to her. But she kept wailing.

I had read how screens were bad for babies, but I was desperate and alone and couldn't take her crying anymore.

So I grabbed Kevin's iPad to search for a baby show on YouTube, hoping it might help soothe her. When I turned it on, I noticed a map app I didn't recognize. It wasn't Waze or Google Maps. I opened it.

It wasn't a map app, after all. It was a decoy—hiding dozens of photos of Kevin with another woman, both of them naked.

Justin-Case97

i need more

Calming4ce_

Same!

Steffed_up

i said it before, and i'll say it again—you're a great writer.

Miz_Beleaf

I have Part Four written but haven't been able to edit it yet.

Justin-Case97

we dont care drop it now

Calming4ce_

Please.

Miz_Beleaf

Out the door now but promise to soon.

Day Five
Wednesday, July 7, 2021

Norma opened her front door and saw Cookie and two police officers sitting in her living room.

"You're sure you didn't know he was married to Jennifer Addis?" the male officer asked Cookie.

"Why would I want to be engaged, let alone have a baby with a married man?" Cookie responded.

"You'd be surprised," the female officer quipped.

"Well, I had no idea. And now that he's dead, I don't know how to begin processing the betrayal," Cookie said.

"What are you going to do about your daughter?" the male officer asked.

"What do you mean?" Cookie said. "We buried her."

The two officers looked at each other.

"Your daughter is alive," the female officer hedged.

"Alive?" Cookie gasped.

"There was a medical error, and she went home with

the wrong parents, whose daughter died," the female officer said.

"She was switched with another baby?" Cookie asked.

"Yes," the male officer said. "The hospital said they contacted you."

"I haven't looked at my messages since Liam was killed," Cookie said, pulling out her cell phone.

Norma approached Cookie and sat down on the couch next to her. Cookie played the message.

"Oh my God…" Cookie said. She turned to Norma. "Rose is alive."

"We recommend you seek legal counsel," the female officer said.

"I'm not going to sue the hospital," Cookie said. "I'm just happy she's alive and that I'll get her back."

"That's not why you need an attorney. The hospital told us the other parents are going to fight to keep her," the male officer said.

"What?" Cookie said. "But that makes no sense. She's my daughter. How can they do that?"

"This doesn't seem fair," Norma said.

"You should call the hospital," the female officer said.

"Thanks for your time today," the male officer said. He stood up and walked toward the front door. The female officer followed him out.

Norma shut and locked the door behind them and returned to Cookie in the living room.

"This is a living nightmare," Cookie said. "I have to fight to get my own child back because of a hospital mistake?"

"I can't believe it either," Norma said.

"I have to return to work immediately," Cookie said. "I need to save money to pay for whatever legal bills I'll have to get Rose back."

Norma suddenly felt the tectonic plates shift beneath her.

While she had supported Cookie returning to work to get over Liam, it was an entirely different matter if the goal was to save money to get Rose back. Cookie and she had finally returned to a good routine, just the two of them. And now, it could all be spoiled by a third wheel.

"Are you sure you want to do that?" Norma asked.

"Do what?" Cookie said.

"Fight to get Rose back?" Norma replied.

"Are you fucking kidding me?" Cookie said.

"I'm sorry," Norma said, even though she wasn't.

Liam was an evil man. He was a cold-blooded killer. God only knew what genetic material he was made of. But of course, she couldn't tell Cookie any of that.

"She's *my* daughter," Cookie continued.

Norma felt Cookie slipping through her fingertips like grains of sand shooting down an hourglass and needed to shut this down fast.

"I'm just protective of you," Norma said. "I don't want to see you go through the pain of an awful legal fight when the outcome isn't guaranteed."

"As opposed to the pain of not having my daughter back?" Cookie said. She shook her head incredulously and rolled her eyes.

The eye roll.

The dreaded fucking eye roll.

If Norma had a nickel for every Cookie eye roll she had had to endure in her lifetime, she would've been a billionaire by now.

Norma felt herself getting triggered and took a breath. She needed to collect herself to find a way to keep Cookie under her roof and persuade her not to fight to get Rose back. "Maybe it makes sense to move in with me to save money instead of wasting it on rent," she said.

"No," Cookie said. "I need my own space to set up a home for Rose. I'm getting my stuff and leaving."

"Now?" Norma asked.

"Yes," Cookie said. She stood up and marched to her childhood bedroom to gather her things.

And just like that, Norma was left in the dust again.

The same way Cookie had abandoned her when she went to day camp for the first time. The same way she had deserted her when she got her first high school boyfriend. The same way she had left Norma behind when she took off for college, never to look back again.

Norma stared at the grocery bag on the laminate kitchen counter filled with Cookie's favorite goodies. The unopened bottle of Martinelli Cider was sweating beads. The plastic bag stuck to its wet neck, and the cork was bulging, begging to be popped open.

Cookie always had a way of ruining everything.

THIRTY-THREE

LIZ

Day Six
Thursday, July 8, 2021

My red-eye flight just landed. I'm walking through the airport, and every television screen is covering the breaking news about Kevin Addis's murder and Jennifer Addis's disappearance.

I'm wearing a baseball cap to hide in case anyone recognizes me. It seems to be working because nobody has stopped me yet.

I exit the airport and catch an Uber to go to the hospital. I debated calling first because there's a good chance nobody there will be willing to speak with me. But I decided not to because there would've been an even smaller chance had I tried by phone.

I'M STANDING in front of Bell Psychiatric Hospital again, staring at the same glass sliding doors. It feels like deja vu.

But it's five days later, and I'm not picking up The Singing Patient this time. Instead, I'm being investigated for helping her escape and possibly kill her husband.

I step in front of the doors. They part like the Red Sea. I sure could use Moses's help right now to guide me out of this mess.

I walk inside the hospital. The same security guard with thick brows greets me again. The one who dropped Jennifer Addis's suitcase in front of my feet, declaring it "safe."

"What can I do for you?" he asks.

"I'm here to see Betsy," I say. The silver sister nurse who brought Jennifer out to me.

"And you are?" he says.

He doesn't remember me. Maybe the baseball cap is working. I wonder if I should lie but decide to tell him my real name because Betsy will probably remember me.

"Liz Blau," I say.

He takes out a walkie-talkie from his pocket when I notice Betsy stepping out of a patient room. She immediately recognizes me despite my hat.

"What are you doing here?" she asks, approaching me.

"I'm trying to find Jennifer Addis," I say. "I'm being falsely accused of helping her run away when I didn't. She's the only one who can clear my name. I'm wondering if you might know where she might be now."

"I saw the video of you in front of the airport bathroom," Betsy says. "It sure looked like you helped her escape."

"That was a fake manipulated video," I say.

Betsy raises her eyebrows. "How about the one of you running a red light near the motel where her husband was killed?"

"I was on my way home from work," I say. "I've never

been to that motel. Do you think I'd come here if I was in on it?"

Betsy shrugs.

"I'm desperate because I'm being accused of crimes I didn't commit. Please, just tell me if you have any idea of where she is."

"Maybe you forgot she never spoke?" Betsy says.

"Do you have any idea why Jennifer Addis might've wanted to run away from here? Did it have to do with her daughter? She had a picture of her daughter taped behind her during her surprise performance on *The Underdog*. I'm sure she missed her while she was here."

"I wouldn't know," Betsy says.

"Is there anyone here who can help me?" I plead.

A loud beeping sound goes off.

"I'm afraid not," Betsy says. "Even if someone heard something here, everything is covered under patient confidentiality."

"Is her doctor around—Dr. Clara Griffin?" I say.

"She has the day off," Betsy says.

"When does her next shift start?" I ask.

The beeping sound keeps going off.

"I need to tend to a patient," Betsy says. "Have a nice day, Ms. Blau."

Betsy walks away and steps inside a patient room. She was way friendlier five days ago when she was excited about Jennifer Addis's prospects on *The Underdog*.

Two patients step out of a room next to the one Betsy just entered. They're chatting and look familiar with each other. Maybe they're roommates. It hits me—what if Jennifer had a roommate here?

I probably wouldn't be given permission to speak with them if I asked. I look over to the guard who stepped out of the hospital and is talking on his phone near the entrance. Betsy is still inside the patient room. Before either can see me, I make a dash for the room where I saw Jennifer Addis walk out five days ago.

I slip inside and quietly shut the door behind me. A young woman with a pixie haircut sits on a bed crosslegged. She's dressed in a gummy bear pajama set and is holding a worn-out teddy bear, missing a few limbs.

"I've been waiting for you," she says.

THIRTY-FOUR

NORMA

Day Six
Thursday, July 8, 2021

Norma had drained an entire bottle of Pinot Grigio by herself and passed out on the couch the night before. She bought the wine in bulk in cases at Costco. After Cookie abandoned her again, she was thankful to have a chilled one ready to get her through the night.

When she woke up in the morning, there was drool on the couch cushion she had used as a pillow. Oreo, who she had retrieved from Cookie's bedroom after Cookie left, was sitting upright and staring at her from the corner of the couch.

The summer sun glared through the window, making Norma's eyes water. Her head felt heavy, and she shuffled to the kitchen to take Advil. After drinking coffee and eating breakfast, her head felt better.

Norma decided that if Cookie was going to leave her for Rose, she wanted no trace of her daughter left in her home and got to work. She stripped the sheets off Cookie's bed and tossed them in the washer. She grabbed a garbage bag and went into the bathroom to throw out anything Cookie might have left behind.

She noticed Cookie had forgotten her toothpaste and toothbrush. And Norma wasn't about to let her know. Instead, she tossed both items in the trash bag, hoping Cookie's breath would smell bad today and that she'd repel people, leaving her feeling abandoned. The same way she had made Norma feel due to her selfish behavior.

Norma noticed the bathroom garbage can was overflowing with Cookie's snotty tissues from crying over that waste of a man. Norma bent over and pulled the dirty bag from the can, replacing it with a new one.

She stood up straight again, tying it into a knot, and caught a glimpse of herself in the bathroom mirror. The bruising on her neck from Liam's fingertips had nearly disappeared. She couldn't wait for all traces of him to be gone.

After finishing up in the bathroom, she returned to the kitchen and opened the cabinet where she had stored Cookie's Hello Kitty table set to throw it out, but she didn't see it. She checked the dishwasher. It wasn't there either.

Norma searched every kitchen cabinet, opening and slamming each one shut. The set wasn't anywhere. It was gone. She opened the utensil drawer, looking for the matching Hello Kitty utensils. The fork and spoon had also disappeared.

The bad feelings returned for Norma.

The fury of one thousand suns.

Norma knew what had happened.

Cookie had *stolen* them.

THIRTY-FIVE

LIZ

Day Six
Thursday, July 8, 2021

"Waiting for me?" I ask.

The woman with the gummy bear pajamas nods her head.

I take a seat on a sheetless twin bed across from her.

"What's your name?" I ask.

"Ruth," she says. "Or Joy. Or Delilah."

"Which is it?" I ask.

She doesn't respond.

"How long have you been here?" I ask.

"A day. Or a month. Or a year," she says.

This is going nowhere fast.

"Were you The Singing Patient's roommate—Jennifer Addis?" I ask.

She smiles at me.

"Did she ever speak with you?" I try.

She keeps smiling.

Is that a yes or no?

Might as well be direct.

"If the nurse or guard finds out I'm speaking with you, I'll be escorted out. I don't know if you have access to the news here. But I'm being falsely accused of helping Jennifer Addis run away when I wasn't involved. I need to find her. She's the only one who can clear my name. Did she ever tell you where she was going?"

"Los Angeles. Or Rome. Or Cairo," Ruth or Joy or Delilah says.

I'm done with the games. I stand up to leave.

"Wait," she says. "Did she do it?"

"What?" I say.

"Kill her husband," she says.

"I have no idea," I say.

"I'm wondering if I was rooming with a murderer."

"Can't help you," I say.

"Heard she tried to poison a bunch of patients before she left here," she says. "Poison?" I ask to make sure I heard her correctly.

She nods and squeezes the neck of her limbless teddy bear. Its limp head falls to the side.

Day Six
Thursday, July 8, 2021

Norma slammed her car door shut and angrily stomped to Cookie's house.

She banged as loudly as she could on the front door, pounding with both of her fists. "Open up!" Norma yelled.

Cookie sure was taking her damn time.

Norma lifted her shoe and kicked the door until Cookie finally opened it.

"I'm here to retrieve my stolen property," Norma said.

"What are you talking about?" Cookie said.

"You stole my Hello Kitty cutlery set and utensil—"

"No, I didn't," Cookie interrupted her.

Norma felt very triggered. Cookie was peeing on her leg while telling her it was raining.

As a teenager, she had done the same thing. Lying to Norma's face over and over again:

"You promised me I could get my belly button pierced!" Cookie had shouted.

"I did no such thing!" Norma had yelled back.

It took everything in Norma's power to remain collected.

"Why would I want a Hello Kitty anything?" Cookie asked Norma.

"Because Hello Kitty is your favorite," Norma replied.

"Hello Kitty is definitely *not* my favorite," Cookie said, cackling. "I'm a grown woman."

Norma could no longer contain her anger. "Don't gaslight me!" she said, raising her voice. "I'm the one who paid for the set, and I want it back now!"

Norma tried shoving Cookie aside. She wanted to go inside the house to get her items, but Cookie blocked Norma with her arms.

A young woman wearing black and white marbled Lululemon pants, pushing a stroller, stopped on the sidewalk in front of Cookie's house, watching the commotion unfold.

"Everything okay?" she called out.

"Not really," Cookie responded.

"Do you need me to call the police?" the woman asked.

Norma glared at Cookie. "You wouldn't dare."

"Watch me," Cookie mouthed back.

Norma turned to the young woman. "No problems here. I was just leaving," she said.

Origin Story

Part Four:

After discovering pictures of Kevin and another woman naked together, I didn't know what to do. I needed to get advice from someone who I trusted. Someone who loved me.

I had already planned to visit my Dad because he was too sick to travel, and I wanted him to meet his granddaughter. I decided to bump up the trip and didn't bother asking Kevin to join because I knew he would say he was too busy with "work" to come.

When I saw Dad, he was very diminished. I felt guilty sharing the upsetting news with him, but he was thankful I did. He reminded me about the fortune I stood to inherit after he passed and told me that even if I filed for divorce immediately, Kevin could drag it out until after he died to get a piece of my inheritance.

Dad said I needed to hire a private investigator and a divorce attorney to find out exactly what was happening with Kevin and get help planning my next steps. He gave me referrals for both.

As soon as I returned home, I hired the P.I. and contacted the divorce attorney too. It didn't take long before the investigator showed me pictures of Kevin and *one* of his mistresses.

The P.I. thought there were more. I wondered if the naked pictures I had uncovered on Kevin's iPad weren't only of one woman. I hadn't looked at them closely because I didn't have the stomach for it, and I didn't have it in me to look at them again.

The investigator said he needed a little longer to get more pictures of Kevin and the other women he suspected he was having affairs with. He offered me the photographs he had to take home. I told him I didn't want them but that my divorce attorney would contact him as needed.

The day only got worse from there. When I got home, I got a call from the hospital. Dad had died. I immediately collapsed on the kitchen floor and wept as soon as I heard the news.

Dad was gone. My marriage was a sham. And I had a newborn.

How would I find the strength to get through this chapter of my life alone?

I didn't have a choice because Juliet needed me.

On cue, I heard her crying.

I took my antidepressant and went upstairs to the nursery to change her. When I lifted her from the crib and put her on the changing table, she swiped at my hand again—and didn't stop.

It took a moment to realize what was going on—I was being attacked. She kept swatting me over and over again.

I backed away from her and tripped. I tried regaining my footing but knocked my head on the corner of the changing table.

The last thought I had before everything went dark was this was it—the moment my baby girl would take me out.

Justin-Case97
mic drop

Calming4ce_
Damn.

Steffed_up
LOVE!

Miz_Beleaf

Y'all are the best. Thanks for your support.

THIRTY-SEVEN

LIZ

Day Six
Thursday, July 8, 2021

I rush out of Jennifer Addis's old hospital room with my head down before Nurse Betsy or the guard, who are talking together in the hall, can see me. I don't look up again until I'm outside.

My phone rings. It's Jeff.

"Hi," I say, picking up.

"Hi," he says. "I have an update. My contact at the LAPD told me the police traced your loan payoff to an offshore LLC bank account in the Cayman Islands. They still haven't determined who the owner of the account is."

"I don't know anyone rich enough to hide money in an offshore bank account," I say.

"I don't think I do either," he says. "As for Kevin Addis, they weren't able to recover enough DNA from the crime scene to put together the killer's profile because bleach was poured all over his motel room."

"Does that mean it was premeditated like someone was trying to cover their tracks?" I ask.

"They aren't sure yet," he says. "My contact also mentioned they uncovered Kevin Addis was leading a double life."

"What?" I say.

"He was having multiple affairs and engaged to a few other women," he says.

"Who?" I ask.

"Their information hasn't been released yet. There's speculation that Jennifer Addis went crazy after she found out Kevin was cheating on her, which led to her being committed until she found a way to escape. They think she might've killed him for revenge."

"Oh my God," I say. "I just heard a rumor she was poisoning patients during her stay at the psych hospital."

"How'd you hear that?" he asks.

"I'm here," I admit.

"At the hospital in New York?" he asks.

"Yes," I say. "I couldn't afford to hire a private detective. I figured coming here was my best chance to get leads because I need to find her. She's the only one who can clear me."

"Leaving L.A. creates the appearance you're running away from something," Jeff says. "And if she killed her husband and poisoned patients at the psychiatric hospital after she was committed, it doesn't sound like you should be anywhere near her."

He has a point. "I won't be here long," I say.

A man and woman dressed in hospital scrubs walk past me.

"That poor baby girl," the woman says. "A killer mother

on the loose and now a dead father. Do you know if she's still staying with the Dad's Aunt?"

"Haven't heard any updates," the man says.

"Maybe the Aunt will adopt her," the woman says.

I'm pretty sure they're talking about Jennifer Addis's daughter.

"I gotta go," I tell Jeff. "I'm meeting my cousin for lunch now."

"As your attorney, I strongly advise you to return to L.A.," he says. "And as someone worried about your safety, I'm asking you to please come back."

"I promise I will soon," I say. "I'm planning to catch a flight back tonight or tomorrow morning at the latest."

"Let's talk soon," he says.

"Sounds good," I say. "Bye for now."

I hang up and do a search for "Kevin Addis Aunt" on my phone. I wonder if she knows where Jennifer is. Several articles pop up about his murder and Jennifer Addis's disappearance, but nothing comes up for his Aunt.

I start to feel light-headed and dizzy and realize I haven't eaten anything since I landed. I need to get to the diner across the street and order food before I pass out.

THIRTY-EIGHT
NORMA

Day Six
Thursday, July 8, 2021

Norma was home alone, sitting on the couch next to Oreo, blowing through a bag of Pepperidge Farm Milano mint chocolate cookies, trying to calm her rage.

After everything she had sacrificed for Cookie, Cookie repaid Norma by *stealing* her Hello Kitty set and *lying* about it afterward. Cookie was even ready to throw Norma under the bus when her neighbor offered to call the police on Norma.

Norma wasn't going to take this lying down, not after dedicating her entire life to Cookie, only to be met with a slap across the face. It was time to turn on the jets.

Norma picked up her phone and dialed 911.

"911, what is your emergency?" a female operator asked.

"I need to report a robbery," Norma said.

"Where are you?" the operator asked.

"At home," Norma said.

"What's the address?" she asked.

"5231 Manhasset Lane, Long Island," Norma answered.

"Are you injured?" she asked.

"No, my daughter stole a family heirloom," Norma said.

"Is she using a weapon?" the operator asked.

"No, but she was very threatening when I went to her house," Norma said.

The operator paused. "You went to her house?" she asked.

"To get it back," Norma explained.

"Is your daughter with you now?" the operator asked.

"No," Norma said.

"You need to go to your local police department to file a report," the operator said. "This line is for emergencies only."

Norma hung up, clipped the top of the Pepperidge Farm Milano cookie bag, grabbed her purse, and drove to her local police station. She waited patiently before a burly officer finally approached her to take down details of what had happened to file a report.

"What are the items in question?" he asked Norma.

"A vintage Hello Kitty set," Norma said.

The officer squinted in confusion, unsure of what to make of this.

"Hello Kitty?" he asked to make sure he understood.

"Yes," Norma said.

"Even if it's a vintage set, I'm not sure it would meet the criteria for petit larceny," he said.

Who was he to tell her what was valuable? She bit her tongue, holding back her fury. "One man's trash is another man's treasure," Norma said.

"How do you know your daughter stole it?" he asked.

"She was staying with me, and after she left, I noticed it was gone," Norma said. "It didn't walk out of my house by itself."

The officer nodded his head, unconvinced. "Unless you have actual proof she stole it, your daughter could sue you for falsely accusing her of larceny. And if you waste the department's time by making officers chase down false charges, you could face charges of your own for filing a false police report."

What a complete waste of time, Norma thought.

She picked up her purse and stormed out of the station.

NORMA WAS BACK at home on the couch with Oreo. The officer had been utterly useless in helping her get her stolen property back.

Maybe someone online could help her. She opened the TikTok app and typed "guidance coach" in the search bar.

"It's not a setback—it's a setup," a male coach with a beard said, wearing a t-shirt with Tequila, Tacos, and Naps printed on it.

"Courage is not the same as fearlessness. It is action in the face of fear," another coach said with a filter turned on that turned her face into a cartoon.

"Anger is a dead end. Start keeping track of the good," a female coach with braids said, who didn't look older than fourteen.

"You'll know <u>exactly</u> what to do when you get there," the final one told Norma, sitting on the ground in some kind of yoga pose with his eyes closed.

The problem was Norma had no idea what to do.

In what universe was it fair that Cookie had gotten

away with a crime against Norma after *everything* Norma had given up for her?

Norma closed the TikTok app and opened the Facebook app. It had been about a year since she had logged on after the Keanu Reeves imposter had tried to fleece her. When she opened it, she noticed a series of messages from Janie that were several months old:

I haven't heard from you in a while. All well? —J

If you need to talk, the group is here. —J

Hope you're doing okay. Thinking of you. —J

Norma felt guilty for not having responded to her old friend's messages, who had been concerned about her. She finally messaged Janie back:

I'm sorry I've been out of touch. I fell into a depression. It would be nice to get together again.

She wondered if she'd hear back from Janie after going dark for almost a year. But to her surprise, Janie got right back to her.

I understand. I can meet anytime. —J

Today? Norma responded.

Yes. Just tell me where. —J

Janie couldn't have been more accommodating. She agreed to meet Norma at a diner near Norma's home. Norma felt regret for not having stayed in touch with her. If anyone could understand what Norma was going through now, it was Janie.

Day Six
Thursday, July 8, 2021

I haven't seen my cousin Charlotte in a decade. She's my Mom's sister's daughter. We grew up in different states and, through the years, saw each other at destination family events like weddings and bar/bat mitzvahs. As adults, we've stayed in touch via social media.

Charlotte is a psychologist in private practice in Manhattan and married with two young kids. When I texted her about my visit, she asked if I was okay, having seen the news coverage about me and The Singing Patient. She invited me to stay with her family in their apartment in NYC. But I don't know how long I'll be here, and I don't want to drag any of them into this mess if the paparazzi following me in L.A. show up here.

I enter the diner, packed with local residents, hospital staff, and patient visitors with sticker name badges on their shirts. I see Charlotte seated in a corner booth. She waves me over. I walk over to her, take off my baseball cap, and we hug each other.

"How are you?" she asks with a worried look.

"I've been better," I admit.

"I'm sorry," she says.

"I just asked the nurse at Bell Psychiatric Hospital if she knows where Jennifer Addis might be because Jennifer's the only one who can clear me of this mess. The nurse was tightlipped, and the doctor who treated Jennifer has the day off. She probably won't tell me anything either, but I'll still try speaking with her before I leave."

"Who's the doctor?" Charlotte asks.

"Clara Griffin," I say.

"Dr. Clara Griffin?" Charlotte asks, surprised.

I nod my head. "You know her?"

"Yeah, I haven't heard her name in years," she says. "She was driven out of private practice in Manhattan."

"Why?" I ask.

"Insurance fraud. There were rumors she had a gambling addiction that she was trying to fund. She was in a big group practice. I have a friend who shared an office with her. I'm surprised she didn't lose her medical license. Maybe the board put her on probation instead of revoking it."

"Even if she didn't lose her license, why would any hospital hire her after that?" I ask.

"There's a shortage of doctors in New York state willing to work in psychiatric hospitals. They're basically hiring pulses at this point. I doubt she'll ever be able to work in private practice again in Manhattan. She was run out of town."

Charlotte and I order eggs and bagels. I drink a cup of much-needed coffee as she catches me up on her family. I'm slightly distracted by the television mounted on the wall above the diner's counter that's airing news coverage about Jennifer Addis's disappearance and Kevin Addis's grizzly ice pick murder.

At one point, the screen fills with a picture of Jennifer Addis's surprise performance on *The Underdog,* with the taped photograph of her daughter behind her.

"Excuse me," I tell Charlotte. "I probably should watch this."

I look up at the television. They've cut back to a reporter standing on the studio lot next to a poster of *The Underdog.* "In a tragic turn in a story that has gripped the nation, baby Juliet, the daughter of Jennifer and Kevin Addis, is now an orphan. Police say she's currently in the custody of his Aunt, Simone Addis."

FORTY

NORMA

Day Six
Thursday, July 8, 2021

"I had no idea Cookie had it in her," Norma told Janie. They were seated at a booth, sipping coffee and eating pancakes.

"What did she steal from you?" Janie asked.

"A valuable family heirloom," Norma replied. "The police discouraged me from filing a report. They said unless I have proof, she could sue me for falsely accusing her of theft."

"How did she take it?" Janie asked.

"We briefly reconciled after her fiancé passed. I mistakenly let her stay with me. She stole it before she left," Norma said.

"Did she have her baby?" Janie asked.

"It's a long story," Norma deflected.

Janie nodded. "I guess you learned that she's not a safe person for you. Maybe she did you a favor."

This rubbed Norma the wrong way. Cookie had not

done Norma any favors. *Ever.* And she certainly hadn't done her a favor by *stealing* from her.

"It doesn't feel that way," Norma said.

"I understand. How's the volunteer job at the hospital going?" Janie asked, trying to change the subject.

"I quit over a year ago after my granddaughter supposedly died," Norma replied.

"What do you mean your granddaughter supposedly died?" Janie said, concerned.

"She was switched with a baby who was born the same day as her that died," Norma said.

Janie almost spit the coffee out of her mouth. "Oh my God," she said.

"It's been very difficult," Norma added. "Another couple took her home."

"Do they still have her?" Janie asked.

"Yes," Norma said. "There's an investigation going on to figure out how it happened. I obviously had nothing to do with it."

Janie looked at Norma strangely, which made Norma wonder if she had accidentally let the cat out of the bag.

Janie picked up her coffee mug, took a sip, and looked around the diner. She seemed eager to focus on something other than Norma and settled on the television screen mounted to a wall above the diner's counter. It was playing news coverage about The Singing Patient's escape and Kevin Addis's murder.

"Have you watched *The Underdog*?" Janie asked Norma.

"Yes," Norma said.

"It's crazy what's going on with that contestant who escaped," Janie said.

Norma nodded and sliced the pancake on her plate.

"The orphan's my favorite," Janie continued.

Norma put her utensils down. "Svetlana?"

"Is that her name?" Janie asked.

"Yes," Norma said.

"I really hope she wins," Janie said. "I think she has the best voice."

Janie was wearing on Norma's very last nerve. She stabbed the last piece of pancake with her fork and stuffed it in her mouth.

FORTY-ONE

LIZ

Day Six
Thursday, July 8, 2021

"I better head back to the city for my afternoon patients," Charlotte tells me. "Are you sure you don't want to stay with us tonight?"

"I need to be near the hospital. I want to talk to Dr. Clara Griffin when she returns for her next shift. I'm planning to return to L.A. right after," I say.

"Let me know if you change your mind," Charlotte says.

"I will," I say. "It was good seeing you."

"Next time, stay longer. For Shabbat," she says. "Join us for Friday night services."

"That would be nice," I say.

I haven't been to temple for too long. So many of my memories there are connected to my Mom. Maybe that's why I largely stayed away after she died due to fears that reminders of her would hurt too much.

We pay the bill and say our goodbyes. Charlotte leaves, and I head to the bathroom at the back of the diner to use before I go. After I wash my hands, I look up on my phone Kevin Addis's Aunt, Simone Addis, which the news coverage mentioned.

Her contact information immediately comes up, and her address isn't too far from the diner. She's as good of a lead as any I have to find out where Jennifer Addis might be until I can speak with Dr. Clara Griffin. I open the Uber app on my phone and request a driver to take me there.

I walk back through the diner to go outside to wait for the car. An older woman in a prairie dress stands up from a booth just as I pass her, and we accidentally bump into each other.

"Excuse *you*," she says, annoyed.

"Sorry," I say.

FORTY-TWO

NORMA

Day Six
Thursday, July 8, 2021

Norma stood up from the booth when a young woman rudely bumped into her. She looked familiar, like someone Norma had seen on T.V. before.

"Excuse *you*," Norma scolded her.

"Sorry," the woman said.

Norma brushed past her and followed Janie outside to the parking lot. Norma had paid for their meal because Janie had driven an hour to meet her.

But now, Norma regretted her act of generosity. Janie didn't deserve a free meal. She didn't deserve a damn thing. First, she had the nerve to tell Norma that Cookie had done her a favor by *stealing* from her. And after, she praised *Svetlana* of all people.

"It was nice seeing you again," Janie said, standing by her black Mercedes. "Stay strong."

What a stupid thing to say, Norma thought.

Miss-Know-It-All thought she had all the answers, so

high on her own supply that she didn't realize she was a dolt or "mid" at best, as Norma had heard the kids on TikTok say.

Norma smiled tightly at Janie. "Likewise," she said. She turned around and walked to her car. Only one good thing had come from their meeting. The conversation with Janie had reminded Norma that a couple was currently in possession of what Cookie wanted most in the world—Rose. Cookie had no knowledge Norma knew who they were nor the damage she could do with that information.

Cecile Strong had mentioned Brooke and Anthony Romano by name when she interviewed Norma at the hospital. Fortunately, Norma's reptilian brain knew to store and remember their names. Norma was proud of her reptilian brain. It was the reason she had survived conditions under which most humans would have wilted and died.

Norma opened her trunk and removed the Yellow Pages phonebook to search for the Romanos' home address, which she quickly located. She wondered if Brooke might remember that Norma had visited her hospital room when Norma was trying to find out why Liam had been there the day before. She worried Brooke might recall that Norma had carried Sadie out of the room, which would directly implicate Norma in the hospital investigation for who switched the two girls, until a memory returned to Norma:

"I was rushed to the hospital and left my glasses at home. I can't see your badge. What's your name?" Brooke had asked Norma.

"Donna," Norma lied because she wasn't sure if she was allowed to be in a patient room.

If Cookie wanted to toy with Norma's life by stealing her property and giving the green light to a neighbor to call the police on her, Norma would meet her daughter with deserved fire. Cookie didn't realize she was no Houdini, and Norma could outfox her any day of the week.

Norma got in her car, turned on her engine, and drove directly to the Romanos with her yellow phonebook riding shotgun.

Posted by Miz_Beleaf

Origin Story

Part Five:

I first heard the beeping sounds. Then, the antiseptic smell hit me. I opened my eyes and looked down.

I was lying on a bed, dressed in a mint green hospital gown.

"What happened?" I asked a female nurse with small teeth and white hair. Kevin was standing next to her.

"I'm going to be your primary nurse here," she said. "A psychiatrist will be in shortly to speak with you."

"I'm in a psychiatric hospital?" I asked Kevin.

"Yes," he said, nodding.

"Why?" I asked.

"Something hasn't been right for a while," he said.

"I just found out my Dad died and collapsed. I don't need to be here," I insisted.

The door swung open. A woman stepped inside.

"This is your psychiatrist," the nurse said.

"We're going to take good care of you," the doctor said.

She looked familiar, but I couldn't place her.

She tucked a piece of hair behind her ear, giving me a fresh view of her face.

That's when it hit me—she was the woman in the pictures with Kevin—the ones the private investigator had shown me.

Justin-Case97
this is gonna be a movie

Calming4ce_

My coworker published a book and has a literary agent. I can put you in touch with him.

Miz_Beleaf
Really?

Calming4ce_
You deserve it.

Steffed_up
who says social media can't be used for good?

Calming4ce_
I'll DM you.

FORTY-THREE

LIZ

Day Six
Thursday, July 8, 2021

I'm standing in front of Simone Addis's house. I ring the doorbell, but nobody answers. Maybe it's broken. I try knocking.

I hear someone approaching the door. "Go away," an elderly woman says.

"I'm here about Jennifer Addis," I say. "It's important."

"Go away," she says again. "You can tell your newspaper boss I'll press charges if you come by again."

She thinks I'm a reporter.

"I'm not a reporter," I say, taking off my baseball hat, looking through the peephole, hoping she can see me. "I'm *The Underdog* chaperone who took Jennifer Addis to the airport when she fled. I'm trying to find her so she can clear my name because I had nothing to do with her disappearance."

The door cracks open with the chain still locked in

place. I see her through the crack. She looks like she's in her seventies and has short white hair.

"I recognize you," she says. "From the video at the airport."

"It's fake," I say. "I'm sorry for coming by without notice. But I never met Jennifer before I picked her up. I've lost my job because of this, and the police are threatening to file charges against me. I need to find her."

Simone drops the chain and opens the door wider. "Sorry, I was rude. The reporters won't leave me alone," she explains. "But I'll tell you the same thing I told them. I have no idea where Jennifer is."

"Is there any chance I can come in to speak with you?" I say.

She sighs and reluctantly lets me in. I step inside her living room and take in the framed photographs hung on the wall of the family from decades past. I also notice several pictures on top of the fire mantle, including a recent picture of her and Kevin at Christmastime.

She notices me looking at the photos and points to one of her when she was decades younger with a little boy. They're both standing in front of the mantle decorated for Christmas with hanging red stockings and pine cones, and he has his arms wrapped around one of her knees.

"That one is of Kevin and me when he was six. I never had kids of my own. He treated me like a second Mom." Simone is all choked up and trying to hold back tears.

"I'm sorry for your loss," I say.

"Have a seat," she says.

I sit down on the couch, and she sits in a lounge chair across from me.

"My nephew tried to do the right thing. Jennifer was very sick. He was terrified of leaving her alone with Juliet.

One of the hardest decisions of his life was committing his wife to a psychiatric hospital. But he did it to protect Juliet."

"I can't imagine," I say.

"After Jennifer escaped, he went to L.A. to try to get information from the show's producers about how it could've happened. He had been against Jennifer doing the show because he didn't think it was safe. I guess he was right. If she hadn't done it, he'd still be alive."

A tear slides down Simone's cheek. She reaches for a tissue box on the coffee table.

"I'm really sorry," I say. "I want you to know I'm not involved in any way with your nephew's death. Jennifer left me twisting in the wind, and now I'm fighting for my life."

"Sounds like her," Simone says bitterly. "I know the media is reporting that Kevin wasn't a saint. How he cheated on her. But I never knew him to be anything other than a wonderful nephew. He mowed my lawn each week and took me to doctor appointments when I needed help. He didn't deserve to die, especially like this."

"Nobody does," I say.

"Juliet is an easy baby. She sleeps a lot like she is now. But I never imagined I'd be left with the responsibility of raising a child at my age," Simone admits. "My nephew had no other living relatives, and Jennifer is a fugitive now. I imagine if they catch her, she'll be institutionalized again or go to prison for a long time. And I don't want to put Juliet in foster care."

"Has Jennifer tried to visit you to see Juliet?" I ask.

Simone shakes her head. "I'm not sure she knows I have Juliet. If she does, she probably knows coming around here wouldn't be a good idea. It's not just reporters that have been by—police have been here too."

"I know you said you don't know where Jennifer is, but

did you ever meet any of her friends or people she was close to who might know where she's hiding?" I ask.

"No. Whenever I saw her, it was only with Kevin and Juliet. I didn't know any of her friends."

Guess I've hit another dead end.

"Thanks for speaking with me when you're going through so much," I say. "I don't want to take up any more of your time." I stand up to leave, and she follows me to the front door.

"I hope your ending is better than my nephew's," she says ominously before shutting the door.

I walk to the corner of her street and call an Uber. I'll wait at the diner near the hospital, where I met Charlotte earlier, until Dr. Clara Griffin starts her next shift, and speak with her then.

There's a fifteen-minute ETA time before the next driver arrives, probably because I'm in a residential area of Long Island. There aren't many drivers around here. I sit on the curb when my phone makes a sound—a text from Jeff:

Headed back yet?

Still need to speak to Jennifer Addis's doctor, I text back.

I hear noise up the block. I look up. It's Simone, hurriedly leaving her house with a large bag slung on her shoulder. She's carrying Juliet. She unlocks her car, straps Juliet in the back, and gets in the driver's side. She turns on the engine and speeds away.

FORTY-FOUR

NORMA

Day Six
Thursday, July 8, 2021

Norma put on a fresh coat of coral lipstick before knocking on the Romano's door. Anthony Romano opened it.

"I'm here to speak with you and your wife about my granddaughter, Rose Butterfly Case," Norma told him.

"We can't speak with you," he said. "You'll have to talk to our attorney."

Brooke, who Norma remembered from the hospital, appeared by his side. "What's going on?" she asked.

"I'm Rose's grandmother," Norma said.

Brooke squinted her eyes at Norma, and Norma wondered whether she recognized her.

"I'm on your side," Norma said. "My daughter isn't fit to be a mother. I want to help you. May I come in?"

Anthony and Brooke looked at each other before letting Norma inside. They motioned for her to take a seat in their dining room.

"My highest priority is my granddaughter," Norma

explained. "My daughter is a very troubled person. Her judgment is lacking. She had a baby with someone who was married to someone else. She cannot be entrusted with the responsibility of raising any child, even if it's biologically hers."

"Is this something you'd be willing to testify about?" Anthony asked.

"Yes," Norma said. "I can also write a letter and meet with your attorney, whatever you think would be most helpful. I just want my granddaughter to be raised by good parents."

Norma's eyes watered. Brooke grabbed a box of tissues from a side table and handed it to Norma. "This is selfless of you to do," Brooke said.

"Doing the right thing isn't always easy, but doing the right thing is always right," Norma said.

"You can leave us your number, and our attorney will definitely follow up with you," Anthony said.

"Of course," Norma said.

"I just put Sadie down," Brooke said. "Otherwise, we'd let you see her."

"Maybe next time," Norma said.

The Romanos both nodded their heads. Norma scribbled her number on a PostIt note from her purse and thanked them for allowing her to visit.

When she got to her car, she smiled, satisfied.

Cookie had *no idea* what she had gotten herself into. She was in a knife fight in a phone booth, blood in her teeth —with Norma—who would win every time.

Norma put her car key in the ignition about to turn it on when her phone made a sound. A text. If it was Cookie coming to her senses, ready to admit she had stolen Norma's property, it was too late. That ship had long sailed.

But the text wasn't from Cookie—it was from an unknown number:

We know you switched the babies. Hand over 50K in cash tonight or we'll turn over our evidence to the police. Location will be texted 30 minutes before.

FORTY-FIVE

LIZ

Day Six
Thursday, July 8, 2021

The driver arrived thirteen minutes after Simone hurriedly left with Juliet. There was something strange about the way she ran off. The large bag she was carrying. How she sped away in her car. She didn't mention a thing about going anywhere when I spoke with her, which is also weird. I wish I could've followed them, but I had no way to do so.

I text Jeff to let him know, suggesting it might be worth contacting the police to do a safety check at the house to make sure all is okay with Juliet. I also tell him I'm on the way to the diner near the hospital where I'm planning to wait for Jennifer's doctor to start her next shift, whenever that is.

It's been a day. I take off my baseball hat, shake out my hair, and pull it back in a ponytail.

"I knew I recognized you," the Uber driver says. He's looking at me through his rearview mirror. "You're the chaperone from *The Underdog.* The one who helped Jennifer Addis escape."

"I never helped Jennifer Addis with anything."

"What about the airport footage?" he asks.

"It's fake," I say. "Someone manipulated it and tried to extort me for 100k before they released it to TMZ."

"Jesus," he says. "This world. I'm Adam, by the way."

"Nice to meet you," I say.

"Why are you here?" he asks.

"I flew in from L.A. to try to find Jennifer because she's the only one who can clear my name. I lost my job because of this mess. But I've come up empty-handed so far."

"I'm sorry," he says. "I've been following the story closely because my parents live in the same town where Jennifer and Kevin had their house," he says.

This piques my interest. "Has anyone spotted her there since she disappeared?"

"Nah," Adam says. "I think she's too smart for that. People would see and report her to the police."

"I figured," I say. "That's why I didn't bother looking into going there."

"It looks like an abandoned haunted house now," he says.

"You know where it is?" I say.

"Yeah, it's a few blocks from my parents' street where I was raised," he says. "I've driven by. The yard is a mess. Mail is overflowing from the mailbox. The postman is probably the only person that's been by there in months. The house sticks out like a sore thumb. My parents told me neighbors have started complaining to their local councilwoman. They're worried about it affecting their property values."

Maybe I should go there. I can't afford another plane ticket back to New York, and I don't want to leave any stones unturned; however unlikely it is, I'll uncover anything. Plus, I have time to kill.

"Can you take me there?" I ask.

ADAM WAS RIGHT. Jennifer's front yard is overgrown with bushes, weeds, and piles of fallen leaves. God knows the last time a gardener was here.

I walk up to the front door and notice the mailbox next to it overflowing with mail. A few envelopes have fallen on the ground. I pick them up and knock on the door. Nobody answers. I open the mailbox to return the envelopes, but it's overstuffed, and more mail falls to the ground.

I notice a few envelopes from the same sender: **Katz Intelligence**. I flash to Vince, mentioning the P.I. firm he wanted me to hire to help track her down: L.A. Intelligence.

I wonder if Katz Intelligence is a private investigator firm too. I look it up on my phone. A Yelp listing immediately comes up—it is a P.I. firm. Wouldn't a private investigator be more discreet than sending correspondence through the mail? The envelopes are all addressed to Jennifer Addis—why did she hire a P.I.?

I turn around and see Adam still waiting for me in his car. I had asked him to keep the Uber tab running. I put up my finger to let him know I need another minute. If Jennifer Addis hired Katz Intelligence, maybe there's a chance they know where she is now.

I call the number listed on the Yelp listing, but it's no longer in service. I do another search for Katz Intelligence.

Another listing comes up on Google with a different number, which I try.

"Hello," a woman answers.

"Is this Katz Intelligence?" I ask.

"Katz Intelligence is closed," she says.

"I have a quick question about Jennifer Addis—"

"Don't call here again," she says and hangs up.

FORTY-SIX

NORMA

Day Six
Thursday, July 8, 2021

Norma drove home in a panic, clutching her steering wheel tightly with her nervous, sweaty palms.

Who sent her the text?

Her first instinct was to go to the police, despite them treating her terribly when she had gone there earlier to file theft charges against Cookie. If whoever was trying to extort her was bluffing, she would have nothing to worry about, and the police could be useful.

The problem was if the extorters weren't bluffing. What *proof* could they have that she switched Rose with a dead baby? Was there someone at the hospital that day who had seen and recorded Norma? It seemed there was always someone around with a phone camera these days. Norma couldn't even go to the supermarket without running into a shopper who was taking a picture of an apple.

What if the extorters had a video of her switching the babies? Then she'd turn into a household name, like *The*

Underdog chaperone, who looked the other way at the airport when The Singing Patient, aka Liam's wife, fled.

Norma was in a serious pickle. This wasn't a scam like the Keanu Reeves imposter who had tried to get her to send him money. Norma *had* switched the babies, and *someone* knew.

She came to the realization that she had no choice but to pay up. But what if she gave them 50K, and they kept wanting more? She didn't have endless reserves of money.

When Norma got home, she opened a fresh bottle of chilled Pinot Grigio and poured herself a hefty glass. She sat on her couch, drinking it and anxiously petting Oreo. She picked him up and hugged him tightly.

Why couldn't people be like Oreo?

She knew in her bones the world would be a much better place if they were.

Her phone was face down on her coffee table and made a sound. She was scared to look at it. What if it was the extorters again?

Courage is not the same as fearlessness. It is action in the face of fear, the TikTok coach said.

She put Oreo down and picked up her phone—another text from an unknown number:

If you don't pay up tonight, an orange jumpsuit awaits you.

Norma's mouth went dry. Her heartbeat quickened. She stood up, ran to her bedroom, and opened her closet door. On the bottom shelf lay her late husband's brown leather briefcase. It was covered in a thick coat of dust.

What would Ray tell her to do now? she wondered.

She picked up the briefcase and blew as hard as she could, releasing a plume of dust into the air.

FORTY-SEVEN

LIZ

Day Six
Thursday, July 8, 2021

Why did the woman hang up as soon as I mentioned Jennifer Addis?

I try calling the number again.

"Hello," she answers.

"I just called about Jennifer Addis—" I say, but she hangs up again.

What's going on?

Something tells me she knows something about Jennifer Addis. Since she won't speak to me on the phone, I need to try to speak with her in person. I look at the Yelp and Google listings, but there's no address attached to either.

The only person I know who might be able to track down an address is Vince since he's a programmer and knows about all things tech. I quickly text him: In NY now. Have a favor to ask. Can you track down the address for Katz Intelligence?

He immediately texts back: Guess the detective work isn't going well. You've finally decided to hire a P.I.?

I don't have a lot of time. An Uber is waiting for me, I text back.

Vince texts me two addresses—a P.O. Box and a residential address, which I share with Adam.

"The house address isn't that far from here," Adam lets me know. "I can take you there, but then I have to go. I need to pick my kid up from school."

"Okay," I say.

We arrive at the residential address associated with Katz Intelligence.

"Good luck," Adam tells me. "Guess I'll hear how this story ends on the news."

"Thanks for your help," I say.

I get out of the car, walk to the front door, and knock. A bereft-looking woman around thirty years old opens it.

"Hi," I say. "I'm Liz. I tried calling Katz Intelligence about Jennifer Addis—"

She tries to shut the door, but I stick my hand between the door and the frame to stop her.

"Please go," she says.

"I was *The Underdog* chaperone," I say. "I'm being wrongly blamed for helping Jennifer Addis disappear. But I never met her before I picked her up. I flew here to try to find her because she's the only one who can clear my name. I was just at her house. Her mailbox was overflowing, and there were several envelopes on the ground from Katz Intelligence—"

I stop myself because the woman just winced when I said 'Katz Intelligence.'

"I told you on the phone it's closed," she says. "It was my late husband's firm. He died not long ago."

"I'm sorry for your loss," I say. "I wouldn't have come here like this if I had known. I thought maybe someone from a P.I. firm Jennifer Addis was involved with might know where she is now."

"Jennifer Addis never paid Neil for his services. After weeks of requesting payment in his usual discreet ways, he sent the outstanding bills to her house."

"Do you happen to know why she hired him? Was it because she suspected her husband was cheating on her?"

"Most women hired Neil for that reason," she says.

"Did your husband ever mention anything that might give me a hint about where she could be now?" I ask.

"No. Sorry," she says and shuts the door.

I guess I've hit another dead end. Time to go back to the diner and wait for Dr. Clara Griffin, who may or may not have information that will lead me to Jennifer. I sit down on the curb and request another Uber.

The gravity of my situation hits me. I don't have a job. I'm likely going to face charges for helping Jennifer Addis disappear. The police also seem bent on trying to connect me to Kevin Addis's murder. I don't know how I'm going to get through what awaits me. It feels crushing and insurmountable. I start to cry.

A door swing opens. I turn around. It's her again.

"Sorry for loitering," I say and quickly stand up. "I'm waiting to be picked up."

"Are you okay?" she asks.

"Not really," I say, swiping the tears off my cheeks. "It's overwhelming to be falsely accused of something you didn't do. The police told me I could face prison time if I'm convicted of helping Jennifer escape."

"I'm not a fan of the police either," the woman says.

"They haven't taken my concerns seriously about Neil's death."

"What do you mean?" I ask.

"I'm Ava," she says. "You can come in."

I follow her inside the house. She leads me to a kitchen table, where I take a seat.

"Coffee?" she offers.

I wonder why she's suddenly being so welcoming. "Sure," I say.

"How do you take it?" she asks.

"Milk, no sugar," I say.

She prepares me a cup and takes a seat across from me. "Sorry I was rude before, but I have my reasons for not trusting anyone connected to Jennifer Addis. Sounds like you've been screwed over by her too."

"What do you mean?" I ask.

"I'm pretty sure Neil's death is because of her," she says.

"Really?" I say.

She nods. "After Neil mailed Jennifer her overdue bills, Kevin Addis contacted him to pay them off, which was strange. Normally, husbands aren't thrilled if they discover their wives hire private investigators to look into their affairs, let alone offer to pay them for their services after the fact. But Kevin told Neil Jennifer had been committed, which is why she hadn't paid him, and that he was in charge of paying her outstanding bills. Looking back, I think Kevin was trying to confirm that Jennifer had hired Neil. A few days after their call, Neil told me he was being followed. When he got a view of the guy, he recognized it was Kevin Addis from the pictures he had taken of him for Jennifer."

"Kevin Addis was following your husband around?" I say.

"Yes, and he didn't stop. It got to the point where Neil

told me he was going to file a restraining order. But then, he was killed in an office fire and never had the chance."

"Oh my God," I say.

"The police said the fire was caused by a cigarette that Neil forgot to put out, but I don't believe them."

"Why not?" I ask.

"Neil never smoked. His Dad, my father-in-law, died of lung cancer, and Neil was terrified of getting it. I think Kevin Addis planted the cigarette in Neil's office."

"Holy shit," I say.

"I don't know if Kevin wanted Neil dead or if he wanted everything inside Neil's office destroyed or both. But I do know that Kevin Addis didn't want the world to find out what Neil had uncovered about him," she says.

"About his affairs?" I ask.

"Neil never told me specifics except that Kevin had been cheating on his wife. I told the police how Kevin had been following Neil around before his death. How Neil had planned to file a restraining order against Kevin. I also told them that Neil didn't smoke. But they dismissed me because of a lack of evidence."

"What about the pictures Neil took? Maybe whoever's in the pictures with Kevin would give police a clue about what he was trying to hide," I say.

"The photographs were all destroyed in the fire," Ava says.

"There weren't digital copies?" I ask.

"Neil was old school. He didn't do anything online. Used the same camera my late father-in-law used, who was also a private investigator. He was the one who trained Neil. Every picture Neil took, he developed himself in the darkroom in our basement."

"There are no pictures there?" I ask.

Ava shakes her head. "It's empty."

"Are you sure Neil didn't keep any pictures anywhere else?" I say.

"I'm sure. We have a safe deposit box at the bank, but he never kept work stuff there. Just our marriage license, birth certificates, a couple of bars of gold, those kinds of things. I haven't been there since he died. Haven't had it in me. The last time I went was eight months after our five-year anniversary trip to Paris to return our passports."

"Is there any chance you'd be willing to go there now just to be sure?" I say. "I know it's a long shot. But if Neil left any work stuff there, maybe there's something about Kevin Addis. Something that might help both of us."

She mulls it over. "People keep getting hurt because of this situation. First Neil, now you," she says. "Let's do it."

"Really?" I say.

She stands up, grabs her car keys from the kitchen counter, and I follow her outside to her car.

FORTY-EIGHT
NORMA

Day Six
Thursday, July 8, 2021

Norma stood nervously in line at the bank, holding her late husband's briefcase. She was waiting for a teller. Only one was working, and two customers were in line before her.

Norma looked around, fearful the extorters might be watching her. Maybe they had followed her to the bank. She was tempted to flee. Run away from all of her problems. To never look back. But where could she go?

"Next," the teller called out, arousing Norma from her thoughts.

Norma walked over to the woman. She had long, manicured fingernails with glued silver rhinestones and a name tag with Alyssa on it pinned to her blouse. "How can I help you?" Alyssa asked.

"I have an odd question," Norma said.

"What's that?" Alyssa said.

"How much money do you think would fit in this?" Norma asked, lifting the briefcase in front of the bandit barrier that separated her from Alyssa. It was special bullet-proof glass designed to protect bank employees. Norma had learned about its bandit nickname from a *Dateline* episode. Unfortunately for her, she was on the wrong side of the glass, and it would do nothing to protect her if bad people had followed her.

Alyssa looked at Norma strangely, lifted her cell phone, and typed something. "According to the internet, a standard briefcase can fit about one million dollars in cash, which weighs about twenty-two pounds," she said.

"One million dollars?" Norma asked, gobsmacked.

"Yes," Alyssa said.

"I don't need that much," Norma said.

"How much do you want?" Alyssa asked.

"Fifty thousand," Norma said.

Alyssa got to work, getting Norma's bank account information and confirming Norma's identification with Norma's driver's license. She pulled out large bills, sorted them into piles, and counted them thrice. Afterward, Alyssa ran each pile of cash through a counting machine to ensure it was the correct amount and repeated the process twice. Once she was sure she had the right amount, she put a rubber band around each pile and slid them through the bottom crack of the bandit glass.

Norma opened her briefcase, took the bundles of cash, and placed them inside.

"Is there anything else I can help you with?" Alyssa asked.

"No," Norma said, locking her the briefcase.

"Next," Alyssa said, smiling tightly.

Norma walked away and toward the bank exit, clutching the briefcase tightly. A television mounted on the wall by the door had the news on. A male reporter standing next to a palm tree in front of a Los Angeles police station was speaking. "Our sources at the LAPD have confirmed that they're getting closer to making an arrest in the murder of Kevin Addis."

A thin older man snuck up behind Norma. "Looks like the ice pick murderer is toast," he said.

FORTY-NINE

LIZ

Day Six
Thursday, July 8, 2021

I'm standing next to Ava as a male bank employee with a buzz cut unlocks her safe deposit box and hands it to her. He points her to a sorting room, and I follow her inside. She locks the door behind us and lifts the top of the box open.

Inside are passports and various legal documents, including Neil's birth certificate, which she holds up. Tears form in her eyes. I gently place my hand on her back.

"Thanks," she says.

She continues going through the items inside the box—gold bars, a very expensive emerald and diamond necklace, and a large diamond ring.

"This was my Mom's," she says, holding it. "She died a couple of years ago. Neil was there for me after she passed."

"I'm sorry," I say. "I lost my Mom too. It sounds like you were lucky to have him."

"I was," she says.

She keeps emptying the box, placing each item on a small

sorting table until the box is empty, except for one small white envelope at the very bottom. She removes it from the box and opens it. Inside are half a dozen pictures of different men with various women in compromising positions.

"Looks like Neil kept a few backup pictures from his old cases here," she says, surprised. "I had no idea."

She shuffles through the pictures until she spots one of Kevin Addis with a woman—who is not Jennifer Addis. She stares at it. "This must be what Kevin Addis didn't want the world to learn about."

Kevin is kissing the woman, whose head is turned to the side. She's wearing a blue bandana and has a large pearl earring in her ear.

"She looks familiar," I say.

"She does," she says. "Like the woman in that painting..."

"Vermeer's *Girl with a Pearl Earring*," I say.

"Yes," she says.

"Can I take a picture of it on my phone? I want to share it with my attorney. He has contacts at the police department. Maybe they can track down who she is."

"Go ahead," Ava says. "I'm going to take it to them right now."

WE JUST LEFT THE BANK, said our goodbyes, and traded phone numbers to share any information. Ava is on her way to the police station now. I'm in an Uber, making one stop before I return to the hospital to see if Clara Griffin has started her shift yet.

I remember Jeff mentioning Kevin was having affairs

with multiple women and engaged to a few women. I check my phone to see if any of their identities have been released yet in case one of them is the *Girl with a Pearl Earring*. But I don't see anything.

I text Jeff: **Any word on the identity of Kevin Addis's mistresses?**

Not yet. When's your flight back? he asks.

Planning to catch one right after I speak with the doctor, I text back.

THE UBER PULLS UP to Simone Addis's house. I want to ask her if she ever saw Kevin with this woman. Maybe she knows who she is, and maybe the woman is a key in Jennifer Addis's disappearance.

Simone's car isn't in the driveway, and the house is dark. Maybe she didn't return after she sped away with Juliet earlier today. Something seemed off when she left.

I get out of the car, walk to the front porch, and peer through the window.

The house is empty.

Everything's been cleared. The furniture. The couch I sat on earlier today. The family pictures on the mantle of Simone and Kevin as a young boy.

Did she move because she was tired of reporters harassing her? It's strange she didn't mention she was planning to move, let alone imminently.

I look her up on my phone to see if she has a forwarding address. But no listings come up for a Simone Addis on Long Island. If she did move, her identity wouldn't have disappeared that quickly unless someone deliberately scrubbed her from the internet because Simone Addis never existed at all.

I flash to the fake Aunt in the television show *The Americans*, who was really a KGB agent who provided cover for Elizabeth's recovery story from a gunshot wound. Was Simone Addis a fake Aunt too? What was the imposter hiding if she was, and where did she go?

My stomach sinks when a far more sinister thought hits me.

Where is baby Juliet?

FIFTY

NORMA

Day Six
Thursday, July 8, 2021

Norma was driving to the address her extorters had texted her thirty minutes before. Ray's briefcase was riding in the trunk with the fifty thousand dollars in cash.

Norma had spent all evening watching the news at home, hoping for an update on who the police had honed in on for the arrest of Liam's murder. The pundits continued with their speculation that Jennifer Addis did it. Norma hoped Liam had traces of Jennifer's DNA on him, connecting her to his murder. They had been married, after all.

Norma pulled into the parking lot where the extorters told her to park. She got out of her car, opened the trunk, and removed the briefcase.

Yes, she felt scared. But she also felt *rage*.

Rage at Cookie.

Norma wouldn't be in this situation if it weren't for her. Norma had switched the babies to spare Cookie a lifetime of having a daughter, who would leave her in the dust the way Cookie had left Norma.

Norma walked toward the alley. She clutched the briefcase in one hand. Her other hand was hidden in the pocket of her prairie dress, holding the bottle of Mace pepper spray. She brought it for protection in case the extorters tried to hurt her.

Her heart thumped so loudly in her rib cage that she thought it might explode. Even though she was terrified, Norma reminded herself she was a fighter. She had survived an assassination attempt. She had raised Cookie alone—

Out of nowhere, a man in a black mask ran up to her and grabbed the briefcase. She lifted her hand from her pocket. Before she could shower his eyes with the pepper spray, he delivered a deadly blow to her head.

Norma collapsed on the cement as he ran away with the money into darkness.

Her body was left splayed on the sidewalk like a crime scene chalk outline from a *Dateline* episode she had watched.

Day Six
Thursday, July 8, 2021

"I think something sinister is going on," I tell Jeff on the phone. "I just found out Kevin Addis's Aunt, if she's real, abruptly moved out of where she was living and took baby Juliet with her. But I'm not sure she's really his Aunt."

"She's not," he says. "After you told me to contact the police for a safety check, they found out the Aunt doesn't exist and discovered the abandoned house. There's a nation-wide hunt underway now for Juliet."

"Oh my God," I say. "I hope she's okay."

"Me too," he says.

"I also found out that Jennifer Addis hired a private investigator, Neil Katz, to look into Kevin's affairs before she was committed to the psych hospital. I spoke with Katz's widow, who told me she thinks Kevin murdered her husband in a staged office fire. She thinks Kevin didn't want anyone finding out what Neil had uncovered about him."

"This is getting too dangerous," Jeff says. "I'm not

comfortable with you being there alone anymore. I'm catching a flight to New York."

Seeing and having him here would be nice, but I don't want to put him out. "I'm not paying you enough to make a special trip," I say, trying to make a joke.

"Too late," he says. "I'm at the airport."

"You *really* don't need to do this," I say.

"I know I don't need to, but I *want* to," he says. "Please be careful until I get there. Stay near the hospital."

"I'm going there now to try and speak with Jennifer's doctor, Clara Griffin. Maybe she knows where Jennifer might've gone."

"I'll text you before I take off," he says.

My other line rings—it's Svetlana. I'd forgotten about her. It feels like five lifetimes ago since we last spoke at the Grove when it's only been two days.

"Thanks," I tell Jeff. "Talk soon."

I pick up the other line.

"Heard you were fired because of the Jennifer situation," Svetlana says.

"Yeah, I was, unfortunately," I say.

"I found out something that might help you. My contact at Christie's came up with three people's names who bought a dark green Tiffany's dragonfly hanging chandelier at auction over the last century. And guess what?"

"What?" I say.

"One of them was Jennifer Addis's Dad. She probably filmed her performance at his house," Svetlana says.

"Where's that?" I ask.

"He died recently," Svetlana says. "His main residence was in Florida."

"I don't think she would've risked flying to another state

with airport security cameras everywhere. She's a wanted fugitive," I say.

"Her Dad also had a summer house in Montauk," Svetlana says.

"That's on Long Island?" I say.

"Yes," Svetlana says. "There's a chance she might be there."

"I'm actually in New York now trying to track her down," I say. "Do you have the Montauk address?"

"I'll text it to you now," she says.

The address immediately comes through on my phone. "Thanks for helping me," I say.

"Good luck," she says.

I need to go there right now. What if Jennifer is there, and what if Juliet is with her too? Maybe Jennifer hired the fake Aunt as a ruse.

***

"YOU GOT FANCY FRIENDS," the female Uber driver tells me as she pulls her Honda in front of Jennifer Addis's father's estate. This is the biggest mansion I've ever seen in real life or on screen.

"Do you mind waiting for me here?" I ask.

"Sure," she says and turns on her car stereo.

I step out and take in the palatial estate. It's perched high on a bluff at the end of the Long Island peninsula. The oceanfront location is buffered by a reserve to the east and the west, making the panoramic ocean views a breathtaking combination of nature and the sea. The lighthouse in the distance and the moon and stars in the sky sparkle on the ocean water below.

The only sounds I hear are waves cashing and music

coming from the Uber driver's car. From the front, the mansion looks completely dark. The glow from the street lights guides me to the front door. I ring the doorbell. Nobody answers. If Jennifer is inside, and especially if she's with Juliet, she must be hiding. Maybe I'll be able to see something from the backside of the estate.

I walk toward one side of the mansion to get to the back, but a large steel gate stops me. I try opening it. It's locked. I walk around to the other side of the estate, but a large hedge that must be ten feet high blocks me. I spot a small opening where it looks like an animal tried getting through. I debate whether to try pushing my body through when a loud *siren alarm* goes off.

FIFTY-TWO

NORMA

Day Six
Thursday, July 8, 2021

When Norma came to, she was lying on the concrete alley and felt something cold on her forehead. At first, she thought it was cement. But when she lifted her hand to touch her face, she realized it was blood. She had a gash a couple of inches wide above her right eyebrow that was bleeding.

She wondered how long she had been lying there. She looked around. The alley was dark and desolate. Ray's brief-case with fifty thousand dollars was gone, along with Norma's jewelry and purse, which had her phone and keys inside.

She needed help, but she couldn't go to the police. Whoever had assaulted her knew that she had switched the babies and had threatened to contact the police with their evidence. She couldn't go to the hospital either because they would probably contact the police.

She had no choice but to walk home alone. She slowly

lifted her bruised body and bleeding head to begin her march back.

BY THE TIME Norma arrived at her front doorstep, she was exhausted. She estimated it had taken her over an hour to walk home, although it could have been more.

She bent down to the planter next to her front door and removed a hidden key to let herself inside. She walked to the refrigerator, pulled out a large turquoise pitcher, and poured herself a tall glass of iced tea to replenish her fluids and electrolytes. She opened a bottle of Advil and swallowed a couple of pills to help quell the radiating pain in her head. She was concerned she might have a concussion.

She took the glass of iced tea, went to the living room, sat on her couch, and hugged Oreo as tightly as she could. If only Oreo could watch over her through the night to ensure she was all right.

Someone needed to make sure she didn't lose consciousness and die. She needed a human being's help—and there was only one person she could ask—*Cookie.*

The saga of the missing Hello Kitty dining set now felt like small fries after being assaulted and left for dead. Norma needed her daughter. After everything she had sacrificed for Cookie, including opening up her home to Cookie after Liam had died, surely her daughter would let bygones be bygones. For once in her life, Cookie would have to be there for Norma. It was the least she could do. Given Norma's condition, she would have to offer her a place to spend the night.

Norma stood up from the couch to call Cookie from her kitchen landline since the extorters had stolen her cell phone. Cookie's line rang, and she picked up. "Hello," Cookie said.

"It's Mom," Norma said.

Cookie immediately hung up on her.

Norma listened to the dial tone in disbelief. Cookie hadn't even given her the chance to explain what had happened. If Cookie knew that Norma had been assaulted, was bleeding, and needed help, she wouldn't have hung up on her.

Norma decided to go to Cookie's house to tell her in person. She needed to spend the night there so Cookie could keep an eye on her.

Norma opened the kitchen salt jar and grabbed her hidden backup car key since the extorters had stolen her keys. She paused momentarily, wondering if she should drive in her condition and without a license since that had also been stolen. Norma realized she didn't have a choice. The stakes were too high. Her life was on the line.

NORMA RANG COOKIE'S DOORBELL. But Cookie didn't answer. It was the middle of the night, and the house was dark. Had Cookie already gone back to sleep after Norma's call?

Norma started pounding on the door with her fist. "I'm bleeding!" she yelled. She kept pounding until she saw a light turn on inside the house and heard shuffling.

Cookie finally opened the door. But as soon as she saw Norma, she shut the door in Norma's face and locked it.

Norma's mouth dropped open. She was stunned. Norma purposefully left the blood on her forehead so that Cookie could see the extent of her injuries. But it didn't seem to matter because Cookie didn't care that Norma was hurt.

"I was assaulted!" Norma shouted through the door.

Cookie didn't open the door again.

"Are you going to let me die on your doorstep?" Norma asked.

Still no response.

"I guess I'll have to wake up your neighbors and ask for their help since you abandoned your elderly mother in this condition," Norma said.

Cookie unlocked the door but only cracked it an inch. Norma shoved Cookie aside and stepped into the house when she saw Cookie's dining room table filled with baby items—for *Rose*.

Norma felt very triggered. Cookie had discarded her in a New York minute and had already moved on.

Cookie noticed Norma staring at the baby items. "Liam and I bought this stuff before Rose was born," she explained. "I've been getting everything ready because I'm going to win her back."

"Are you going to ask what happened to my face?" Norma said, pointing to the blood on her forehead.

"To be honest, I don't want to know," Cookie said.

Norma felt the wrath of a volcano erupting inside of her. Red-hot lava gushed through her veins. She was a bull, and Cookie was the Matador's red cape. After *everything* she had sacrificed for Cookie, Cookie didn't care she was hurt.

Anger is a dead end, the TikTok coach said.

"Anger is a dead end," Norma repeated out loud, trying to calm herself down.

"What are you talking about?" Cookie asked.

Norma let out a long, loud breath before speaking. "I

was assaulted. I might have a concussion, which means I could die if left unchecked."

Cookie stood silently.

Norma inched toward her face. "Are my pupils dilated?" she asked.

"I don't think so," Cookie said, backing away. "I need you to go now."

"Why are you doing this?" Norma asked.

"I've been working really hard to learn to establish healthy boundaries in therapy—"

"No," Norma said, remembering what Janie had told her—the only useful thing that bitch had done. "You've been brainwashed. Therapy is a for-profit business that markets itself to millennials by looking for made-up reasons for parental estrangement. It's your generation's version of repressed memories. As your mother, I must let you know you've been used. I learned this from my support group on Facebook, Mothers of Estranged Daughters—"

A piercing sound suddenly filled the room—a *crying baby*.

Norma looked around, confused. "Who's that?" she asked.

Cookie didn't answer as the baby's cries grew louder.

"What's going on?" Norma pressed.

Cookie still didn't respond.

Norma pushed past her daughter and moved through the house. The baby's cries guided her until she reached a door. She swung it open and saw Rose in a crib.

Norma ran back to the living room. "What you have done, Cookie?" she said.

"I hired someone to pick her up," Cookie admitted, nervously biting down on her lip. "They just dropped her off."

"You hired someone to kidnap Rose?" Norma said.

"I'm leaving town with her. We're going to start over somewhere else," Cookie said. She grabbed a suitcase near the dining room table that Norma hadn't noticed when she first arrived. Cookie started packing the baby items from the table. "I'm sorry I took the Hello Kitty dining set, but I need it for Rose. I hadn't gotten around to buying her one yet."

"The police will find you," Norma said.

"No, they won't," Cookie said.

"Yes, they will," Norma said.

"I'll change my name," Cookie said.

Norma realized Cookie was far gone. Deep in delulu land. She had to find a way to get through her stubborn daughter's thick skull. "You're not going into witness protection," Norma said. "The government isn't providing you and Rose with fake I.D.s. You'll both be all over the news—"

"But she's my daughter!" Cookie shrieked, pounding her fists on the table.

"I know," Norma said. "But you have to go through the legal system to get her back, or you'll end up in prison."

Cookie sat down at the dining room table. She pushed a pack of Huggies diapers to the side that fell on the floor, laid her head on the wooden table, and wept.

Norma approached her daughter and put her hand on Cookie's shoulder. She was the only person in the world who could help Cookie. "Let me make this right for you," Norma said. "I'll drop Rose off at the fire station anonymously."

Cookie couldn't stop crying. Finally, between sobs, she whispered, "Take her."

NORMA RUSHED OUT of Cookie's house, popped open her trunk, and took out a car seat. She placed it in the back-seat, waiting for Cookie to come outside with Rose. Norma's injuries felt like distant memories now. She was turbo-charged and invigorated, given the new twist of events.

When Cookie emerged from the house, she was carrying Rose, who she had swaddled in a blanket. "You got her a car seat?" Cookie asked Norma. Norma nodded and didn't mention it was for Oreo, who had accompanied her on errands and medical appointments.

"Thank you," Cookie said. "Hopefully, you'll be able to use it again after I get her back."

Cookie turned to Rose, blinking tears away, and kissed her goodbye. "Until we meet again," she said, handing her to Norma.

Norma buckled Rose inside the car seat, closed the passenger door, and walked to the driver's side. She turned on the engine and drove to the nearest intersection.

Instead of hanging a right toward the fire station, she turned left and went straight home.

FIFTY-THREE

LIZ

Day Seven
Friday, July 9, 2021

I run back to the front of the mansion and get inside the Uber. The driver blasts music that drowns out the estate's siren alarm, which I must have triggered.

"Nobody's here," I tell her. "Please take me to Bell Psychiatric Hospital."

I sit in the backseat, nervous that a camera caught me. But then, I realize if Jennifer Addis is there with or without Juliet, she wouldn't report me to the police because she's a fugitive.

I text Jeff about Svetlana's tip regarding the Tiffany lamp spotted in Jennifer Addis's performance that her father purchased and explain she might be hiding out at his Long Island mansion with or without Juliet. He immediately texts me back: About to take off. I'll tell my contact at the NYPD.

I'm glad he is because I don't want to go to the police. They won't believe me since they think I'm involved in this mess. I might have a better chance by speaking with someone at the hospital.

"YOU NEED TO LEAVE," the guard tells me. "It's way past visiting hours."

I'm standing next to him inside the entrance of Bell Psychiatric. "I need to speak with Nurse Betsy. I have important information about where Jennifer Addis and her daughter might be," I say.

"Nurse Betsy is off work," he says. "Come back in the morning."

"Is Dr. Clara Griffin here?" I ask.

"Not yet," he says.

He's not going to get rid of me so quickly. "Jennifer Addis's daughter, Juliet, was supposedly staying with Kevin Addis's Aunt Simone, but Simone Addis doesn't exist," I explain. "I thought the imposter kidnapped Juliet, but now I think Jennifer could be hiding Juliet at her father's estate in Montauk."

The guard looks at me like I'm crazy. "This is the last time I'm going to warn you. You need to leave, or I'll physically escort you out myself." He points to the sliding glass doors.

I walk outside. Maybe I should call Charlotte and stay at her apartment in the city until Jeff arrives. I glance at my phone. It's 1:37 am. I don't want to wake her or her family up. I decide to go to the 24-hour diner across the street, where I had breakfast with her earlier, and wait there.

"You again," a woman says. I look up from my phone. It's Jennifer's roommate with the gummy bear pajamas, standing by the side of the building, smoking a cigarette.

"Are you allowed to be out here?" I ask.

"Snuck out," she says, smiling. "Guess what? I found out how my old roomie was trying to poison people before she left."

"How?" I ask.

"Oxy pills," she says.

"Oxycodone?" I clarify.

She nods her head and puffs on her cigarette.

I know about pain medication like oxycodone from my physical therapy days. It's a highly addictive opioid prescribed for acute cases of pain. How in the world would Jennifer Addis, as a patient, have had access to those pills at a psychiatric hospital, and why would she want to kill other patients with it?

"Glad she didn't try to kill me," the roommate says. She takes a final drag from the cigarette, drops it on the ground, and smashes it with her gym shoe. "Cya," she says, sneaking in the hospital's side door.

I walk through the parking lot toward the diner when I see a car pulling into the lot. It's an odd hour for anyone to arrive here unless it's an emergency. Maybe a family is bringing a relative to be admitted at this late hour.

The car stops. A woman in blue scrubs gets out carrying a water bottle and lunch bag. She's a hospital employee. It takes me a second to recognize her as Dr. Clara Griffin, Jennifer Addis's doctor. She's about to start her shift.

I walk toward her to tell her what I think is happening with Jennifer and Juliet. She doesn't see me because she just opened her trunk and stands behind its lid. She takes out a large bag, which she places on the ground, and sifts through it, searching for something, until she pulls out a blue bandana. She returns the bag to the trunk and shuts it.

She pulls back her hair with the blue bandana and turns to the side when I see the pearl earring.

It's *her*.

The woman from Neil Katz's picture—the one Kevin Addis was kissing.

The *Girl with a Pearl Earring*.

Origin Story

Part Six:

It wasn't a coincidence. I had ended up in a psychiatric hospital where one of Kevin's mistresses was a doctor, which could only mean one thing—I was in danger.

There was a reason I had been brought there. God only knew what plans she and Kevin had for me.

"I need my phone to call my attorney," I told her.

"I'm sorry, but electronic devices aren't allowed," she said.

"I want to see my daughter," I said.

"That's not possible right now," Kevin said, standing next to her. "You're a danger to Juliet."

I wanted to scream at the top of my lungs and let the entire hospital know he had been absent for close to a year because the two of them were having an affair. But I'd get labeled as crazy, and they would restrain and sedate me.

The only thing I had going in my favor was that it seemed like neither Kevin or her knew I was aware of their affair. If they found out, I'd be in even more peril.

I decided not to speak at all. It was the only guarantee that I wouldn't, in a moment of anger or carelessness, accidentally let it slip that I knew about their relationship.

Over the next couple of weeks, every day, when the nurse came in with the pills Kevin's mistress had prescribed me, I nodded obediently, put them in my mouth, and pretended to swallow them.

After she left, I spat them out and covertly hid them in a hole inside the bottom of my bed mattress without letting my room-mate see.

After a few days of being unmedicated, something strange happened. My mind was clearer, and I felt more in control than I had during my entire pregnancy and in the months after.

I flashed to the antidepressants I had been taking during that time. Kevin was the one who had always picked them up for me from the pharmacy. It was the *only* thing he had done for me for a year.

Had he and his mistress doctor switched out the medications my doctor had prescribed with something to cause me to have a psychotic break?

Soon after I stopped taking the medication at the psych hospital, patients started getting really sick. I overheard conversations between worried relatives and administrators discussing the situation. The hospital started doing mold tests. Carbon monoxide detectors were installed in each room in addition to the ones in the hallway.

But I was okay.

Once, when Kevin arrived for his fake weekly visit, I temporarily broke my silence to tell him I thought I should return home since the hospital wasn't a safe place. Patients were getting sick.

He said he didn't feel comfortable with me being at home with Juliet since "my doctor," aka his mistress, had not cleared me for discharge.

After he left, I stormed into my room, upset, and found my roommate with her hand stuffed in the mattress hole where I had hidden my pills.

"I've been passing them out," she said, smiling. "People can use a lil extra help around here."

That's when I realized—this is why patients were getting sick. Kevin and his mistress doctor were trying to make me ill *or worse* with whatever she had prescribed me that my roommate was giving out.

"You need to stop," I warned her. "It's dangerous."

"I'll be gone soon, anyway," she said. "Got my ticket out of here. My sister's gonna record me singing and submit my audition to a new show called *The Underdog.*"

Justin-Case97

i need moorrree pleazzz

Calming4ce_

This is SO good. My coworker said you haven't contacted her yet about her agent.

Miz_Beleaf

I'm planning to after I finish the entire thing.

Steffed_up

can't wait for the next installment.

FIFTY-FOUR
NORMA

Day Seven
Friday, July 9, 2021

Norma walked down the creaky steps, holding Rose, who was thankfully sleeping.

The basement was a relic of a past forgotten chapter: Cookie's childhood.

Now, it would be Rose's new home. Unlike Cookie, Norma had no plans to allow her granddaughter to be part of society. Her biggest regret was ever letting Cookie participate in public life, who had repaid Norma in kind by leaving her in the dust countless times.

Norma had learned her lesson the hard way. And she would never make the same mistake again. Rose would be *all* hers. For eternity. She would keep Rose in her basement, off the grid, until the end of time.

Fool me once, shame on you. Fool me twice, shame on me.

Norma didn't need a TikTok coach to give her that advice. She had *lived-in* experience. She could make her own TikToks if she wanted. And maybe she would. She had so much to teach the world. The sky was the limit. She had proven she could do *anything* over and over again.

The other upside to Rose being off the grid was Cookie would find herself alone again. She would have nobody in this big bad world except for Norma, which meant Cookie would need and appreciate her mother like she never had before.

Norma reached the basement's only closet, where she had stored Cookie's crib decades before. She opened the closet's door and deposited Rose in the crib, who woke with a piercing cry—an awful *high-pitched shrill.*

Norma had forgotten how much she hated the sound of a crying baby. When Cookie was an infant and wailed, her cries didn't make Norma feel powerless the way she had heard other mothers describe their children's cries made them feel. Cookie's screams had been reminders of Norma's dashed dreams, suffocating her until she could barely breathe.

"A baby girl will steal your beauty," someone cautioned Norma before Cookie was born. But they failed to warn her that Cookie would steal her life too.

Norma picked up Rose from Cookie's crib to comfort her. She was wailing, and her mouth was wide open. Norma spotted a small white bump on Rose's bottom gum. She was teething. And drooling. Her gums were dripping with bacteria-filled saliva. Norma also noticed beads of moisture stuck between the skin folds of Rose's neck. She smelled terrible too—like poop.

Norma swallowed her disgust and carried Rose around the basement, bouncing her up and down, trying to console her. But Rose kept crying.

Norma returned her to Cookie's crib and grabbed one of

Cookie's old pacifiers. The pacifier's clear plastic had faded to a brown manure color, but its shape remained intact. Norma tried handing the pacifier to Rose, who promptly swatted it away right into Norma's eye.

Norma grabbed her eye in pain and left the closet to return upstairs. She went to the bathroom, shut the door, and splashed cold water on her eye. When she looked in the mirror, she noticed blood on her forehead from the alley incident and wiped it off.

Even with the water running and the bathroom door closed, Norma could still hear Rose's unnerving cries from downstairs.

The bad feelings returned for Norma.

There was no denying it.

She had an unfortunate case of buyer's remorse.

Day Seven
Friday, July 9, 2021

I'm seated on a chair in the waiting area of a police station near the hospital. I wasn't planning to come here, but I need to speak with an officer now after what I just discovered.

Jennifer Addis's doctor, Clara Griffin, was Kevin Addis's mistress. What are the chances of that being a coincidence? Close to none. Is this why Jennifer was trying to escape from the hospital? Who knows what Clara and Kevin possibly had planned for her there?

Is this why Kevin didn't want anyone to find out about Clara and him? Why he might've killed Neil Katz, who knew the truth? I text Ava to tell her what I've uncovered and that I'm waiting to speak with the police about it. She immediately texts me back: Hope you have better luck than me. They dismissed me when I showed them Neil's picture.

I text Jeff, share what I've learned, and let him know I'm at the police station. He doesn't respond. Maybe there's a Wi-Fi issue on his plane.

A short, stocky officer approaches me. "Officer Johnson," he says. "Come with me."

I follow him out of the waiting area to a small room, where we both sit down. I get right to it. "Have you heard of Jennifer Addis?" I ask. "The Singing Patient?"

"Yeah, we're working her case," he says. "I recognize you from the airport footage."

"It was manipulated," I say. "I never helped Jennifer run away, but I think I know why she might've wanted to escape the psychiatric hospital."

"Why's that?" he asks.

I point to the picture on my phone's screen—the one Neil Katz took of Kevin Addis kissing Clara Griffin on the cheek. "The woman in this picture is Dr. Clara Griffin. She was Jennifer Addis's doctor at Bell Psychiatric Hospital, where Jennifer's husband, Kevin Addis, involuntarily committed her. This photograph shows that Kevin and Clara were having an affair. I don't think it's a coincidence that she was also Jennifer's doctor. Jennifer Addis's roommate at the hospital told me that Jennifer was supposedly trying to kill patients with pain pills before she fled. But I have a different theory. I think it might've been Clara Griffin."

"I'm not following," Johnson says.

"Opioids are typically used for pain management. Even if the psychiatric hospital had a supply, how would a patient like Jennifer Addis have had access to them? I think Dr. Clara Griffin might've made it seem like Jennifer Addis poisoned other patients as a pretext to permanently commit her or maybe to get her arrested so she could have Kevin all to herself."

"Kevin Addis is dead," Johnson says.

"This happened before he was killed," I say.

"Bell Psychiatric called us when patients started getting sick there. They were doing an internal investigation and asked the department to help them. Dr. Griffin was very cooperative. You're right that Jennifer Addis didn't poison patients with pills—it was her roommate."

"Her roommate?" I ask, confused.

"Yes," he says. "Jennifer Addis's roommate stole pain pills and secretly passed them out."

"That's not what she told me," I say.

"A patient at a psychiatric hospital lied to you?" Johnson says. "What a shocker. And we met with Dr. Griffin after Kevin Addis died. We interviewed all of the women he had affairs with. He used different aliases with each one. None of them knew he was married, including Dr. Griffin."

"You believe her?" I say. I remember what Charlotte told me. "Do you know about her history of insurance fraud due to a gambling addiction? Is this a trustworthy person?"

Johnson raises his eyebrows. "You're one to talk?"

"I already told you. I had nothing to do with Jennifer Addis's disappearance," I say.

"Look, we investigated all of this. Dr. Griffin and Kevin Addis met at Gamblers Anonymous. We confirmed it with the leader of their meeting. When we interviewed Dr. Griffin, she was devastated to find out the truth about the man she loved. Kevin knew she was a doctor, but he didn't know where she worked.

"Why wouldn't he know that?" I ask.

"I don't think he was interested in the details of his mistresses' lives. That's not why he was with them. After he involuntarily committed Jennifer to Bell Psychiatric, we assume he learned Dr. Griffin worked there because the hospital visiting logs show he never visited his wife when

Dr. Griffin had a shift. He deliberately avoided Dr. Griffin discovering the truth about his life."

While I'm no detective, I'm not buying it. Kevin probably didn't visit the hospital when Clara was working to avoid any outward slips of appearance that the two of them were having an affair. Clara Griffin was Jennifer Addis's doctor at a psychiatric hospital and was also in a relationship with Kevin Addis. The P.I., who was on to their relationship, mysteriously died in an office fire. It defies common sense that this is all one big coincidence.

I planned to tell Johnson Svetlana's tip about where Jennifer may be hiding. But now, I'm not going to. Because I think Jennifer Addis is in danger, and it seems like Johnson has decided that Clara is an innocent bystander in all of this. If the police find Jennifer now, they'll return her to Bell Psychiatric. Clara will probably find a way to eliminate her as quickly as possible, thereby sealing *my* fate because Jennifer is still the only one who can clear me of any involvement with this case.

Shit. I just realized I texted Jeff the tip about where Jennifer might be hiding. He said he would reach out to his contact at the NYPD about it. I hope he hasn't yet. I quickly text him again, explaining the new turn of events, and ask him not to. He doesn't respond. It must be a Wi-Fi issue on the plane.

I leave the police station, unsure of what to do next. I can't confront Clara Griffin at the hospital. She'll never admit the truth. Maybe someone close to her knows more about what Kevin and her were up to. If they know anything at all, they'd probably want to protect her and wouldn't share it. I do a search for her on my phone anyway. Various articles come up about her medical insurance fraud scam.

I look her up in the white pages. A listing for her comes up that includes a RELATED TO bar with a few of her living relatives. There are few examples of family members turning on their relatives. The only case that comes to mind is the Unabomber's brother.

Maybe if I explain to one of them that a detective has already been killed in this mess, and Jennifer might be next, it would persuade them to open up to me or the police if they know anything. I click on the first name, Clara's mother:

Norma Griffin: Age 60+ / Long Island.

r/TheSingingPatientFanFic
Posted by Miz_Beleaf
Origin Story

Part Seven:

"*The Underdog*?" I asked my roommate. "What's that?"

"People say it's going to be the new American Idol. But for TikTok. I'm going to audition. My family is coming today to record me."

My roommate didn't know that I also had a good voice. Kevin and I had met at a Karaoke bar where he claimed to be bowled over by it.

At the time, I shared with him that I had always dreamt of becoming a singer, which he supported until we got married. After, he said it wasn't a career conducive to having a family and me being a Mom.

Now, I wondered if maybe, like my roommate, my voice could be my ticket out of the psych hospital.

When her family arrived for their visit, I saw them recording her singing in the cafeteria. I seized the moment and started singing too. Maybe someone would notice and record me and submit it to the show.

I sang a cover of Cher's *Believe* like my life depended on it. Everyone, including the hospital staff, nurses, doctors, and patients, stopped in their tracks and huddled around me. I noticed someone in the back of the cafeteria recording me.

A few days later, a producer from *The Underdog* arrived at the hospital. A TikTok of me singing had gone viral. One of the show's producers asked for permission for me to do the show. Kevin's mistress doctor refused to grant it, but the hospital board overruled her because the show promised to pay the hospital a large fee, which the hospital needed. It was also a good P.R. opportunity for the hospital.

After, Kevin tried to stop me from doing it by refusing to grant me permission as my designated healthcare agent. But by that point, the board had allowed me to contact my attorney. I couldn't explain to him what had happened with Kevin and his mistress doctor because she was around when I made the call. But my attorney filed paperwork on my behalf to get the green light for me to do the show.

The show was a ruse, of course. A way for me to escape.

I needed to get out of there to contact the P.I. to get the photographs of Kevin and his mistress, proving she was my doctor too. I also needed to speak openly with my attorney about what I suspected had happened before and after I was hospitalized with the medications they had given me.

They had drugged me to make me go crazy to institution-alize me at her workplace, where they tried to do away with me for good. But they hadn't succeeded. I was still alive. And I was determined to make sure it stayed that way—for Juliet.

Calming4ce_

Whatever happens with Jennifer Addis in real life, promise us a happy ending.

Steffed_up

the world needs more happy endings, for sure.

Justin-Case97

hard agree

Miz_Beleaf

I promise.

FIFTY-SIX

NORMA

Day Seven
Friday, July 9, 2021

Norma was in the basement feeding Rose, who was seated in Cookie's old highchair and eating like a champ. The chair was decades old and had a few tomato sauce stains from spaghetti meals Norma had served Cookie when she was a toddler. The high chair's white-colored plastic had faded to yellow, but it remained sturdy when Norma unfolded and snapped it back into place.

Norma pureed a couple of summer peaches she had picked from the tree in her backyard. With each spoonful, Rose finally seemed to be calming down.

The music also helped. Norma had an old transistor radio with a cassette player in the basement. She plugged it in, put in her Elvis Greatest Hits cassette, and played *Treat Me Nice* for Rose, both to serve as a warning and a sound piece of advice.

She knew Rose couldn't understand the song yet. But she was confident that over time, her granddaughter would learn what it meant. As the lyrics explained, Norma would be nice to Rose *to a point*. The days of being a doormat like she had been for Cookie were over. Done. Finito.

Norma stuck another spoonful of peach mush in Rose's mouth when she heard a loud knock on her front door. It was probably Cookie, who had been a sobbing mess the night before, all up in her fee-fees, as the TikTok kids said. Of course, Cookie needed more comfort from Norma.

Until Norma got a sound machine for the basement to drown out any noises Rose made, she couldn't risk anyone coming inside her home. She would make an excuse to bring Cookie to her backyard.

Norma picked up Rose from the high chair, took her to the closet, and returned her to Cookie's crib. "Time for a nap. No crying," she said, wagging her finger.

Norma walked upstairs and shut the basement door behind her. The knocking on the front door wouldn't stop. "Cookie—is that you?" she called out.

"Hello," a woman said, whose voice Norma didn't recognize.

Norma looked through the peephole. It was the woman from the diner. The one she thought she recognized from television. Why was she at Norma's house?

When Norma opened the door and got a full look at her, she remembered who she was—*The Underdog* chaperone who had looked the other way as The Singing Patient, aka Liam's wife, fled the airport. Norma recognized her from the video she had seen on the news, like the rest of the country.

"Hi," the woman said. "I'm Liz Blau. I came here because I think your daughter might be involved in Jennifer Addis's disappearance."

FIFTY-SEVEN

LIZ

Day Seven
Friday, July 9, 2021

"What are you talking about?" Clara Griffin's mother, Norma, asks me.

I waited at the diner until 7 am before coming here. I still haven't heard from Jeff. He should be landing any minute. I'm sure I'll hear from him soon.

"Do you know who Jennifer Addis is?" I ask. "The Singing Patient?"

"Yes," Norma says. "I recognize you from the video."

"May I come in?"

"This isn't a good time," she says. "I'm getting ready to leave for a doctor's appointment."

An elderly man next door opens his front door with a dog on a leash. "G'morning," he says.

"Good morning," Norma says.

"I think it's better if we speak somewhere more private," I say.

"Fine," she says, annoyed. "My house is a mess. Follow me to the backyard."

She leads me to the back and motions for me to sit on a deck chair next to her in front of a peach tree.

"Do you know that your daughter was having an affair with Jennifer Addis's husband?" I say. I take out my phone and show her the picture of Kevin Addis kissing Clara's cheek, which she pushes away.

"My daughter was *engaged* to him," she says. "She found out from the police after he was killed that he was leading a double life. I don't know what you're trying to stir up here, Ms. Blau, but I have no interest in seeing the man's face who broke my daughter's heart."

"I'm sorry," I say. "I wouldn't have come here if—

The sound of a crying baby interrupts me.

"Who's that?" I ask.

"What are you talking about?" she says.

"A baby's crying," I say.

"I don't hear well due to my advanced age," she says, pointing to her ears. "I have an appointment this morning with an audiologist to get hearing aids. That was the doctor's appointment I told you about. I'm hoping we can wrap this up."

The baby keeps crying.

"I hear a baby. It sounds like it's in distress," I say.

"This neighborhood is filled with families," she says. "There are a lot of children on this block."

I doubt the old man next door had a baby in his house unless it's his grandchild. Maybe it's coming from the house on the other side of Norma's. I stand up and walk through the yard toward it when I spot a small window with opaque glass at the bottom of Norma's house, facing the backyard. I move in front of it, and the baby's cries get louder.

"I think the baby might be inside your house," I tell her.

"That's crazy," she says.

"Do you mind if I check?" I ask.

She shrugs. "Suit yourself," she says. "I was picking peaches out here earlier this morning. The kitchen patio door should be open."

She stays behind in the yard. I open the door, go through her kitchen, and walk toward a hallway where the cries grow louder until I reach another door. It sounds like the baby is behind it.

I crack the door and see a staircase leading down to a basement. The baby sounds like it's downstairs, crying its heart out. I turn around to get Norma, but she's standing right behind me, smiling.

"You surprised me," I say, startled.

"Sorry, didn't mean to," she says before *pushing me down the stairs*.

FIFTY-EIGHT
NORMA

Day Seven
Friday, July 9, 2021

Norma stood at the top of the staircase, staring at Liz, who was at the bottom, wondering if she was dead. Liz's body looked like Liam's did after it had gone still.

Liz had slid down the stairs until her ankle got caught on one, lunging her into the air. She flew several feet before landing on Norma's basement floor with a loud thud. Ironically, the commotion seemed to calm Rose, who had stopped crying.

Norma quietly walked down the steps. She didn't want to stir Rose or rouse Liz in case Liz had only temporarily lost consciousness. When Norma reached the bottom, she bent down and lifted Liz's wrist to check for a pulse—it was still there. She was alive, and it was only a matter of time before she woke up.

Unlike Rose, who hadn't been on the grid long before Norma took her in, Norma couldn't hide this woman in her basement for eternity. Liz had a life. A job. People would be looking for her.

If only Rose had stayed quiet.

Once Liz heard Rose crying and asked to go inside Norma's house to check, Norma had no choice but to let her. If Norma hadn't, she would've contacted the police or some child welfare agency to do a check.

What could Norma do now?

She had to find a way to get rid of her.

But how?

Liz's cell phone was sticking out of her purse, which had fallen off her shoulder after she landed on the basement rug. Norma quickly grabbed both, ran upstairs, and locked the door behind her.

She went to her kitchen, opened a cabinet, reached for a wine glass, and removed a chilled bottle of Pinot Grigio from the fridge. She knew what she needed to do. But first, she needed some liquid courage to follow through. She poured a generous glass, drained it in one swoop, and poured another.

Norma thought about what Liz had said before Norma had pushed her down the stairs. How Liz thought Cookie was involved in Jennifer Addis's disappearance. What had she meant by that?

Norma could follow up with Cookie to ask, but she didn't want to know. Cookie only seemed to know how to get herself in trouble. First, with that loser imposter of a man. And after, by kidnapping Rose. Norma was tired of cleaning up Cookie's messes. She had spent her *entire* life doing that. It was time for Cookie to deal with the consequences of her actions without Mommy coming to her rescue.

Time is a thief, Norma had heard people say about

getting older. But in Norma's case, *Cookie was the thief.* She had stolen Norma's best years, and Norma was DONE.

It was Norma's turn now to put herself first. To finally become who she had always been destined to be. To dazzle. To shine. She wasn't about to let Cookie or the woman in the basement get in her way.

Rose started crying again, pulling Norma out of her thoughts. She finished off another glass of Pinot Grigio, rolled open her utensil drawer, and stared at the ice pick.

Posted by Miz_Beleaf

Origin Story

Part Eight:

I ditched *The Underdog* chaperone at the airport. I felt bad about it, but my life was on the line.

More than anything, I wanted to be with Juliet, but I knew I couldn't return home to see her because Kevin would turn me over to the hospital and his mistress doctor.

The hospital had given me my phone and wallet for *The Underdog,* and I had a hundred-dollar bill hidden for emergencies inside my wallet that I used to catch a taxi at the airport. I headed directly to Dad's summer beach house on Long Island.

I didn't have the house key, but I remembered Dad always kept an extra one underneath a large rock by the gravel next to the fountain in front. It was still there.

I let myself in and looked around. I thought about Dad and all my childhood memories with him there. I wanted to break down and cry. I missed him and needed him more than ever. But there was no time to waste.

I looked up the P.I. I had hired on my phone to contact him about getting the pictures of Kevin and his mistress doctor. My attorney would need to give them to the police as evidence that my husband and her had drugged me and tried to kill me at the hospital. But the first links that came up for the P.I. weren't listings for his firm—they were newspaper articles about him dying in an office fire.

I didn't know what to do without those pictures. I called my attorney and told him everything. He said he couldn't communicate with me without reporting it to the police because I was considered a fugitive. He told me law enforcement would find me. I was national news. I turned on the television, and he was right. Every news station was covering my story.

He said he'd be right by my side if I turned myself in. I told him I couldn't until I could find a way to prove to the police that Kevin and his mistress had planned to kill me. I begged him to follow up on any possible leads and connections between Kevin and the doctor at the psych hospital and, most importantly, to make sure Juliet was okay. He said he would.

There was no food at the house. I created a DoorDash account using Dad's name and a backup credit card he always kept in a kitchen drawer. I couldn't safely go to the supermarket without being recognized, and the likelihood of a food delivery person knowing who owned Dad's house was small.

I got my food, which I barely tasted because I was terrified someone might find me. I kept watching the news, which only made me feel worse.

The chaperone from *The Underdog* who had picked me up was being blamed for helping me escape. I felt horrible and guilty for involving her in my mess. I prayed for her sake and mine that one day, I'd get the chance to explain why I had fled and ask for her forgiveness.

It took everything in my power not to call Kevin to try and hear Juliet in the background. I grabbed a bottle of Pinot Noir from Dad's cellar and poured myself glass after glass until I passed out.

The next morning, I woke up, and it was the Fourth of July. I still couldn't stop thinking about Juliet. And worrying. She was with a monster who wanted to do away with me, *her mother*, so he could live his happily ever after with his mistress.

In a weak moment, I impulsively called Kevin. I planned to hang up right after I heard Juliet in the background. I just wanted to make sure she was all right. But my call went directly to voicemail.

I went upstairs and recorded myself singing in one of the bedrooms with the curtains drawn. I had a picture of Juliet in my wallet and taped it on the wall behind me. I belted out *I Won't Back Down* by Tom Petty to let the world know I would do everything in my power to get Juliet back and away from those sociopaths. After, I created a junk email and sent my recording to *The Underdog*.

It was late. I could hear fireworks lighting up the sky outside but didn't dare to open the curtains. I prayed to God that one day, I'd be able to watch fireworks with my baby girl.

Part Nine:

I woke up the following day, turned on the television, and learned the breaking news—Kevin was *dead*.

And they were tying his death to *me*, but I could've cared less. All I could think about was Juliet—*who had her?*

I kept watching, waiting, and praying for any news about my baby girl. But it never came.

As the day wore on, I couldn't take it anymore. I called a taxi in the middle of the night to go to my house to see who was there with her. There would be less chance of anyone noticing me coming and going at that late hour.

When I arrived, I saw the lawn was a mess, mail overflowed from the mailbox, and Kevin's car was gone. I didn't have a key. I cased the house and peered in the windows.

Nobody was there, including Juliet.

Justin-Case97

wow this is so real

Steffed_up

very.

Calming4ce_

Almost like the real Jennifer Addis could have written it.

r/TheUnderdog

Posted by Calming4ce_

Is it HER???

I'm starting to think Miz_Beleaf is Jennifer Addis.

Justin-Case97

same

Calming4ce_

Remember how she first went viral at the psych hospital, singing Cher's BELIEVE? Maybe her r/ username is an Easter egg.

Steffed_up

what do we do?

Calming4ce_

Call the police.

Steffed_up

what if that gets her in more trouble?

Justin-Case97

maybe we should ask first

Origin Story

Part Ten:

When I returned to Dad's house, there was more breaking news. Someone had killed Kevin in a Los Angeles motel room. Rumors swirled that I was involved with the help of *The Underdog* chaperone.

But there was still no news about Juliet.

The next couple of days were torture, watching the news, desperate for updates about my baby girl that never came. The only thing that got me through that time was the wine in Dad's cellar.

I had finally reached the end of my rope. I was going to turn myself in to the police so I could ask about Juliet.

But then, a reporter on the news mentioned she was staying with Kevin's Aunt. The problem was Kevin didn't have any aunts, or at least none that I knew of.

I looked up the woman's name that was mentioned, found her address, and visited her house in the middle of the night. When I arrived, it was dark. The streetlights guided me as I looked through the windows. The house was empty—no furniture, no people, and no Juliet.

Calming4ce_
It's you, isn't it?

Justin-Case97
she's not gonna tell us if it is

Steffed_up
we're rooting for you.

FIFTY-NINE
LIZ

Day Seven
Friday, July 9, 2021

"May the One who blessed our ancestors — Patriarchs Abraham, Isaac, and Jacob, Matriarchs Sarah, Rebecca, Rachel, and Leah..." Rabbi Weiss says. He's standing on the bema, reciting a prayer, and I'm standing beside him.

I look out at the temple congregants seated below us in the sanctuary —friends, relatives, Dad, Mom—MOM IS ALIVE!

Our eyes lock, and she gives me the proudest smile. I smile back at her and look down at my shoes. They're the black patent leather Mary Janes I picked out for my bat mitzvah.

My bat mitzvah?

I stare at my feet. They're smaller than my usual size seven...because I'm twelve, and I'm at my bat mitzvah.

"Bless and heal the one who is ill: Elizabeth Blau, daughter of Pearl and Zachary Blau. Merciful one, restore Liz, heal her, strengthen her, enliven her—

Wait, Rabbi Weiss is reciting the Mi Sheberach—the Jewish prayer for the Sick—and he just said my name.

Why is he talking about ME?

"Send her a complete healing—healing of the soul and healing of the body, together with all who are ill—soon, speedily, without delay; and let us say: Amen!"

My eyes pop open to white fuzzy static like I'm watching an old broken television set.

Where am I?

I'm not at my bat mitzvah anymore.

The fuzzy static slowly comes into focus and transforms into white, bumpy pieces of cement. A seventies-style popcorn ceiling probably filled with asbestos. I'm lying down, staring at it.

A memory comes firing back: I was pushed down a flight of stairs before everything went dark. The pain hits all at once. Like I've been kicked around for days. Everything hurts. My ankle is throbbing. My head feels like a heavy brick.

I try turning my neck to its side. My cheek touches a shag carpet. I can still move my neck, which is a good sign. But it aches like hell.

I try to stand up. I can't. Every cell in my body vibrates with pain.

I stare at the popcorn ceiling, wondering how long I've been lying here.

A high-pitched cry suddenly fills the room. The sound of a distressed baby. The baby I was trying to find before Norma Griffin pushed me down the stairs.

Why did she push me?

I will myself up again. This time I succeed, because I'm worried about the baby.

I stumble around like a drunk, even though I haven't

had a sip of alcohol in days. I might have a concussion. I need to be seen by a doctor ASAP if I can get out of here. I look on the ground for my bag and phone to call for help. But they're both gone. She took them.

The baby keeps crying. The high-pitched sounds turn into guttural wails.

I make my way through the basement, trying to find it. The basement is like an end times bunker filled with everything needed to raise a child until they reach adulthood. But all of it is vintage—several decades old.

There's one small window the size of a shoe box by the ceiling with opaque glass. The window I must have spotted when I was with Norma in her backyard, trying to figure out where the sound of the crying baby was coming from.

There's only one door down here. I inch toward it. The baby's cries grow louder. The baby is behind the door. I turn the knob slowly, scared and unsure if someone else is inside. When I open it, I see a baby girl alone, lying in a crib, crying her heart out.

My Apple Watch makes a sound. I forgot I had it. My brain is all fuzzy. Why did Norma take my phone and not my watch? Maybe she didn't notice it, or maybe she didn't realize I could communicate with it.

I enter the closet and shut the door so she can't hear me. I try calling 9-1-1, but there's no reception. I step out of the closet and try again, but it still doesn't work.

I notice a bunch of texts. The first one is from my roommate Stefanie:

This will sound crazy, but I think the real Jennifer Addis is posting on r/TheSingingPatientFanFic under Miz_Beleaf. You need to check it out.

The next text is from Jeff:

Just landed at JFK and read your texts. Had Wi-Fi problems on the plane. Please meet me in front of the hospital in 30. FYI Kevin Addis's fiancé's name was finally released: Dr. Clara Griffin. Her mother, Norma Griffin, is going to be arrested for his murder. She was staying at the Heartbreak Motel when he was there. A neighboring building's security camera caught her leaving Kevin's room wearing gloves and carrying his wallet.

I text Jeff back, but it probably won't go through:

I'm in her basement with a baby. She pushed me down the stairs. Send help NOW!!

I hear the door unlock at the top of the stairs—it's her again.

She's come back for me.

I scan the basement for any kind of protection and spot an old broom.

SIXTY

NORMA

Day Seven
Friday, July 9, 2021

Norma drained the entire bottle of Pinot Grigio before returning to the basement with the ice pick. Her kitchen phone wouldn't stop ringing, but she ignored it.

She had bigger fish to fry—mainly, the pesky chaperone from *The Underdog,* who had inserted herself in Norma's plans. Norma swung the basement door open and looked at the bottom of the stairs. But Liz wasn't lying on the ground anymore.

"Hello," Norma called out as she walked down the steps. She scanned the entire basement. Liz was nowhere to be found. Norma heard Rose crying in the closet. The horrendous high-pitched sound that drove her mad. Liz had to be with Rose. She had probably locked both of them inside of the closet.

If Liz thought she could play a cat-and-mouse game with Norma, she would learn quickly and harshly what it meant to lose to Norma.

Norma walked up to the door. "Come out," Norma instructed her.

Liz didn't respond.

"We can do this the easy or hard way," Norma warned.

Liz still wouldn't budge. She was as bad as Cookie. Defiant. Unruly. *Disobedient.*

"I'm going to count to three," Norma said. "One, two, three…" Norma lifted the ice pick and *stabbed* it through the door. Liz screamed, and Rose cried even harder.

Norma felt relief. She was taking control of an uncontrollable situation. Restoring order. Reinstating the correct hierarchy of the universe.

Norma dislodged the ice pick and stabbed it in a different part of the door. Liz kept screaming, and Rose was carrying on too. But Norma felt exhilarated and continued stabbing the door over and over again with admirable focus and determination. By the end, she left it looking like a shredded slice of Swiss cheese filled with holes. Nothing short of a triumph.

Until the basement started *shaking.*

At first, Norma wasn't sure if what she was feeling was real. But when she looked at Cookie's high chair, she saw the bowl with peach puree vibrating on the tray.

What's going on? Norma wondered. An earthquake—*in New York?*

She quickly ran upstairs.

SIXTY-ONE

LIZ

Day Seven
Friday, July 9, 2021

She just stabbed an ice pick through the closet door over and over again. The baby and I are okay. I'm holding her in the back of the closet. As soon as I heard Norma walking back down the steps, I grabbed the broom, locked the baby and me inside the closet, and pushed the crib to the front to try to stop her from getting in.

I think I just heard Norma walk up the stairs and leave the basement. I move the baby to my hip and try calling Jeff and 9-1-1 again from my watch. But my calls still don't go through. I'm too scared to leave the closet to try.

I'm going to need God and prayer to get me out of this. I haven't been inside of a temple in too long and not often enough since Mom died.

God, I'm not ready to die yet. I want to live. I want to make my film. I want to fall in love again. I want my second chance. Maybe even with Jeff. Please have mercy on me and this innocent baby I'm holding. She deserves to live too.

I kiss her on the head and hold her tightly because she won't stop crying.

I just felt the closet vibrate for a few seconds. Now, it stopped. Maybe an airplane passed overhead. It starts vibrating again. This time, it doesn't stop.

I try to listen carefully. Something may be circling above the house.

A helicopter, maybe?

Day Seven
Friday, July 9, 2021

When Norma reached her kitchen, it was vibrating. She wondered if there was a belated thunderbird air show for the Fourth of July. She looked out the window above the sink but saw nothing in the sky.

The kitchen phone wouldn't stop ringing. It had been ringing non-stop for as long as Norma could remember. She finally picked it up.

"Hello," Norma said.

"Hello," Cookie said. "I've been trying to call. Why didn't you pick up?"

"Sorry," Norma said. "I was in my garden and didn't hear it."

"I just checked with the fire station," Cookie said. "No babies were dropped off last night."

"What do you mean?" Norma said.

"I spoke with the person in charge of their Safely

Surrender program," Cookie said. "She's not there. What if someone kidnapped Rose after you dropped her off?"

"I doubt anyone would be brazen enough to kidnap a baby from a fire station," Norma said.

The loud sound outside wasn't letting up.

What in the world was going on?

"I'm going to file an anonymous missing person's report for Rose at the police station," Cookie said.

"I wouldn't do that," Norma said.

"Why not?" Cookie asked.

"The person you spoke with was probably ill-informed. Don't poke the bear, or you could end up in the crosshairs of her kidnapping," Norma said.

"You mean *you* will end up in the crosshairs of her kidnapping," Cookie said.

"No," Norma said. "You're the one who told the officers you were going to fight to get Rose back. You'll be the first person they question."

Cookie started cackling.

"Why are you laughing?" Norma asked her.

"I knew you wouldn't be able to help yourself," Cookie said.

"What are you talking about?" Norma said.

"The baby in your basement isn't Rose," Cookie said.

"I don't have a baby in my basement," Norma said.

"It's Juliet—Liam's *other* baby. The one he had with Jennifer Addis," she said. "We hired a woman to take care of her and pretend to be his Aunt when he went to Los Angeles. The woman dropped Juliet off with me last night. And now, she's *all* yours."

Cookie was laughing maniacally now. The realization hit Norma like a freight train—*her daughter had set her up.* Norma could hardly form words in a state of total shock.

"You always said you were smart enough to be a doctor. Guess you're not that smart," Cookie said.

"I...I sacrificed everything for you," Norma struggled to get the words out. "How could you do this to me, Cookie?"

Cookie stopped laughing. "I am *not* a fucking COOK-IE!" she shouted. "I am DOCTOR Clara Griffin, and I *hate* cookies!"

"It was a nickname," Norma said.

"Then you should've nicknamed yourself because you're the one who likes cookies—*not me*, you selfish bitch," Cookie said.

"Selfish?" Norma said in disbelief. "You named Rose after Liam's dead birth mother and gave her BUTTERFLY as a middle name instead of Norma."

"Thank God I did because after I win my legal fight and get her back, I'll never have to think about you again for the rest of my life," Cookie said.

This cut Norma deeply.

Death by a million paper cuts.

"You cost me *everything*," Norma said. "My hopes. My plans. My destiny. I should've been the doctor—*not you*. You only became one to steal my dream!"

"I didn't steal anything from you. You only have *yourself* to blame for your failed life. I just heard about a grandmother who graduated from Stanford with her Masters degree at a hundred and five years old. Nobody stopped you from doing anything. You didn't become a doctor because you don't have what it takes."

"You only succeeded because of ME!" Norma said.

"No, no, NO!" Cookie shrieked at the top of her lungs. "I did it all on *my own*. Four years of medical school, three years of residency—"

"You had everything handed to you on a golden platter,"

Norma barked back. "Tuition costs covered. Living expenses funded. You're a nepo baby. *I'm* the underdog—"

"You're no underdog. You're just a sad, pathetic *wannabe*. I'm the doctor—something you'll *never* be."

"Apparently, not a very good one—accused of insurance fraud because of a gambling addiction and driven out of private practice to work in a mental hospital," Norma fired back.

"It's true. I was a little low on cash. At least I'm 50K richer now," Cookie said.

"You didn't," Norma whispered.

Cookie didn't respond.

"You hired someone to extort and assault me?" Norma asked.

"The hospital contacted me about their suspicions that you switched Rose with a dead baby. I decided to find out if it was true. Glad I got my answer."

"I only did it to protect you so you'd never have to feel the pain I've had to endure having a daughter like *you*."

"Try having a psychopath as a mother who tries to split up her daughter and her fiancé. Liam and I ran into the actress you hired. She confessed to everything and felt horrible about being a pawn in your sick scheme. I hired her to pay us a visit at The Cheesecake Factory. She was glad to have the chance to pay you back for making him look like a cheater."

"Liam was a cheater," Norma said. "Or should I say, Kevin?"

"Don't call him that!" Cookie shouted. "He was Liam to me. He had plans to change his name legally to Liam but never got the chance to because of *you*."

"Jesus Christ. Listen to your pitiful self, carrying on about a deadbeat imposter who not only lied to you about his name but was also married to someone else and had a kid with them."

"You're very ignorant," Cookie said. "Jennifer Addis threatened to divorce him if he didn't have a baby with her because she wanted a family. He couldn't get out of the marriage until her father died, or he wouldn't have gotten the money he was entitled to in the divorce."

"You knew about her and still wanted to be with him?" Norma asked, aghast.

"He was the love of my life, and you *murdered* him. Even though the police haven't proven it yet, at least you'll be going to prison now for child abduction and trafficking," Cookie said.

As soon as the words came out of Cookie's mouth, Norma realized Cookie must have known about Liam's plan to do away with her in Los Angeles.

"I just called the police with an anonymous tip that you have Juliet in your house," Cookie added. "I'm in my car on my work break, on a burner phone, which I'm about to destroy after I hang up. Good luck in your orange jumpsuit."

"I'm not the only one going to prison," Norma said.

"What?" Cookie said.

As usual, Cookie hadn't thought things through. Whether Cookie wanted to admit it or not, Norma was the smarter of the two. Always a few steps ahead of her daughter. Always able to see the bigger picture that Cookie had failed to grasp.

"Liam's other baby may be in my house," Norma said. "But your DNA is all over her too. On the blanket you swaddled her with last night. On her cheek where you kissed her goodbye. I'll make sure the police know so they can collect your DNA samples."

Cookie got quiet.

"Didn't they teach you genetics in medical school?" Norma said, twisting the knife some more.

Cookie still didn't respond.

"Or maybe you weren't paying attention that day," Norma piled on.

"Don't do this," Cookie said.

"Whom the gods destroy, they first make overconfident," Norma said.

"Rose needs me," Cookie pleaded.

"Rose needs a mother who isn't a criminal. And patients need doctors who aren't delinquents. I'm pretty sure felons aren't allowed to practice medicine in prison. You'll be just like me there. Orange jumpsuit twinsies."

Norma hung up on her daughter. She heard banging in the basement, and Rose wouldn't stop crying. The sound above the house was almost deafening.

"Norma Griffin, step outside NOW," a speaker bellowed from outside.

She looked out her kitchen window again. This time, she saw a helicopter circling above.

She walked to the front hallway and looked in the mirror. The bruises on her neck from Liam's fingers were finally gone. She took out her coral lipstick from the embroidered patch pocket of her prairie dress, put on a thick coat, and smiled in the mirror to ensure she didn't have any on her teeth.

She walked to the front door and opened it up. A crowd had amassed. Reporters, police, and bystanders.

Everyone was there for her.

After a lifetime of being overlooked for a younger, brighter version of herself and stuffing down her dreams while watching Cookie's star ascend, the world finally had its eyes on Norma.

They were interested in what *she* had to say and what *she* had done.

Norma stepped outside and waved at her adoring fans.

Dozens of reporters shouted over each other, trying to win her affection and attention:

"Did you switch your granddaughter with a dead baby?"
"Why did you kill Kevin Addis?"
"Where is baby Juliet?"

"I'm so happy to see you all here," Norma said. "I look forward to sharing my story soon."

A few police officers approached her. A tall one with muscular arms read her her rights.

"Norma Griffin, you're under arrest for the murder of Kevin Addis. You have the right to remain silent. Anything you say can and will be used against you in a court of law. You have a right to an attorney. If you cannot afford an attorney, one will be appointed for you..."

He fastened the metal handcuffs on her wrists. A sea of camera bulbs flashed in her eyes, temporarily blinding her. She readjusted her focus and stood up taller.

She had been waiting for this moment her entire life.

She smiled wide for the cameras.

She was ready for her close-up.

SIXTY-THREE

LIZ

Day Seven
Friday, July 9, 2021

I just heard loudspeakers outside calling for Norma to step out of the house. It must be the police. Maybe Jeff got my messages. Maybe God answered my prayers. Maybe the baby girl and I are going to live. I'm still holding her in the closet.

Suddenly, I hear a swarm of people storm the basement.

"The closet!" a man yells.

The closet's doorknob is busted from the outside. I watch the inside knob fall to the ground. A tall male officer swings open the shredded door with the ice pick Norma used stuck in it. A group of officers and FBI agents stand with their guns drawn.

"Don't hurt me!" I say. "She kidnapped us."

"You're safe now," the officer says. He pushes aside the crib, which I had propped to the front of the closet to protect us. He ushers the baby and me out and upstairs to the backyard—when I see her.

Jennifer.

She runs up to us, takes the baby girl from my arms, and weeps. That's when I realize I've been holding Juliet. I couldn't see Juliet well in the picture Jennifer had taped behind her during her surprise performance on *The Underdog*.

"Is she okay?" Jennifer asks me. "Are you?"

"Yes," I say.

"Thank you for keeping her safe," she says. "I'm sorry for everything. I had to run away at the airport. They were trying to kill me."

"I know," I say.

"I paid off your student loan," she says. "You told me you had gone to The American Film Institute on our ride to the airport, so I had my attorney see if you had any outstanding debt. I know it won't make up for what you've been through, but it's something."

She's the one who paid it off. Although I wouldn't have chosen this way, it's done, and I'm thankful. But I'm more grateful to be alive.

"Thank you," I say.

Jeff walks into the backyard. As soon as he sees me, he runs up to hug me. "Thank God you're okay," he says.

"I didn't know if I was going to make it," I admit. "Did my messages go through? Is that how you and the police knew we were here?"

"The messages came through," he says. "But the police already knew Juliet was here. They got an anonymous tip that Norma was hiding her in the basement," he says.

"Who knew?" I ask.

"Clara Griffin," he says. "She used a burner to make the call, but the FBI was able to figure it out through a voice recognition program. She's in all of this too."

Like mother, like daughter.

"The police will want to speak with you to get your account of what happened," he says. "I'll be right by your side."

"Thank you," I say.

I look around. Police officers, FBI agents, and reporters fill the backyard. Jennifer is off to the side by the peach tree, holding Juliet and smiling through her tears. The helicopter circling above begins flying away. This nightmare may be finally over.

SIXTY-FOUR

LIZ

Nine Days Later
Sunday, July 18, 2021

I'm back at the Grove for *The Underdog* finale. The three finalists—Svetlana, Nolan, and Jennifer—are all performing tonight. The audience will be voting live to decide who'll win.

After the police rescued Juliet and me from Norma Griffin's basement, Jeff took me to a hospital on Long Island. A doctor diagnosed me with a minor concussion but told me to expect to make a full recovery. Jeff and I flew back to Los Angeles together a couple of days later.

I was in touch with Dad the entire time, who repeatedly thanked Jeff on the phone for helping me. Dad offered to fly to New York, but we were leaving for Los Angeles imminently. I told him it would be better if he met me in LA, which he did. He spent the last week here and flew back to Chicago yesterday.

After I returned home, Doug asked to meet at the studio. He gave me a heartfelt apology and offered me my job back. Even though the show ends tonight, *The Underdog* has already been picked up for a second season, and I need this job.

I walk up to the red velvet rope where Svetlana, Nolan, and Jennifer, who's holding Juliet, are standing. C.J. is on the stage, revving the audience before their performances begin.

"Who's excited for our top three tonight?" he shouts. The audience responds with thunderous applause. "Tonight, all of you get to decide this season's winner of *The Underdog,* who will win the two hundred thousand dollar prize and a record deal with Anthem Music Group!"

"Glad you got your job back," Svetlana tells me. "And that you're okay."

"Thanks for helping me," I say.

She nods and smiles.

"Can I get another picture with you?" Nolan asks me. "You're kind of an icon now. You survived Norma Griffin's basement."

"Sure," I say.

I stand next to him by the red velvet rope. He takes a selfie of us together and posts it across his social media platforms with the caption: ICON.

Jennifer, who's still holding Juliet, turns to me. "Would you mind taking her while I perform?" she asks. "You're the only person I trust."

"Of course," I say. "I'm glad you could make it tonight."

Honestly, I'm surprised she's here after everything that's happened.

"I want to show Juliet that she can do anything with her life," Jennifer says. "That she can chase her dreams. Like you did by going to AFI."

"Thanks," I say.

"Are you interested in making films?" she asks.

"I wrote a script I hope to direct one day," I say. "I haven't had the chance to yet."

"Time for our first contestant!" C.J. announces from the stage. "Your favorite orphan...Svetlana Kovalenko!"

Svetlana walks up the steps with the help of a security guard, using her fake walking stick. She's wearing a T-shirt with YOU GO GIRL printed on it. The music starts, and she performs *Lean on Me*. She looks right at me when she gets to the part about leaning on her if you need a friend. I mouth back, thank you. She finishes the song, and the audience stands up to applaud. C.J. runs back on the stage, "Svetlana, everyone!"

I scroll on my phone through *The Underdog's* social media platforms. Gaging by the comments, the love for her remains real:

God bless this young girl.

lawd have mercy

That high note though...AMAZING!

C.J. is already onto the next performance. "*The Underdog's* second finalist and the only guy in our final three... Nolan Jett!"

Nolan runs up to the stage, channeling Elvis in a black leather jacket with the collar up and thick sideburns on each side of his face. The music starts, and at first, he stands still in front of the microphone. This feels different than his other performances when he danced and gyrated all over the stage. He sings *Can't Help Falling in Love* and moves slowly across the stage, extending his arm and offering his hand to various women and tween girls, who scream and offer him their hands back. When he finishes the song, the audience stands on their feet again and applauds. I do my professional diligence and check the social media responses:

MY NEXT SNACK
Convinced he's only singing to me...
It's giving baby Bruno Mars

Nolan runs off the stage, down the stairs, and smiles at me, "Hot guy summer," he says.

Svetlana turns to me, "He's trying to get all girl votes, so Jennifer and I split the rest, and he wins."

"Have you thought about what you'll do if you lose?" I ask her.

"I'm already fielding endorsement opportunities because of the show," she says.

"Really?" I say.

"Yeah, I'm filming a Ray-Ban sunglasses commercial next week," she says.

"Congratulations," I say.

"Now the performance the world has been waiting for," C.J. announces from the stage. "The one, the only, Jennifer Addis...The Singing Patient!"

Jennifer turns to me. "Can you take Juliet now?" she asks.

"Yes," I say. "Good luck." She hands her over to me and walks up to the stage. I position myself in front of her so Juliet and her can see each other. She sees us and blows Juliet a kiss.

The music starts, and it's *Tomorrow, Tomorrow*. From the first line, Jennifer infuses the performance with a sense of hope that the promise of tomorrow still exists no matter what one is facing today. I think about what she must have gone through being committed to a psychiatric hospital without cause by her husband and his mistress doctor, who were both trying to kill her; all the while, her baby girl remained in jeopardy. She gets to the final note and holds it for as long as she can before triumphantly lifting her arms in the air. The entire audience erupts into a standing ovation. She takes a bow, runs off the stage, and takes Juliet from me. "What did you think?" she asks.

"Listen to them," I say, pointing to the audience still standing and clapping. I take out my phone. Someone already posted a TikTok of the performance. The comments are filled with praise:

Literally weeping.
The Singing Patient is finally free…
Never underestimate THE UNDERDOG!

C.J. returns to the stage and asks the three performers to join him. They all walk up, including Jennifer, who's holding Juliet. "*The Underdog* family wants to thank every one of you for an incredible season," C.J. says. "We have exciting news to share…we've been picked up for a second season!" The audience applauds excitedly.

"If you're interested in auditioning, please visit our website and make your voice known. Now, for the part you've all been waiting for…" He holds up a gold envelope, opens it, and removes a silver card. "The winner of season one of *The Underdog* is Nolan Jett!" he shouts. Confetti floods the stage. Nolan captures it all on his phone. Jennifer hugs Svetlana. They both wave to me, smiling, from the stage.

I WALK toward the parking lot to catch an Uber back to my apartment. I'm giving it a week before I start driving again due to my concussion.

"Need a ride?" a guy behind me asks.

I turn around. It's Jeff. He's smiling—the same smile that made my heart skip when I met him at his office for the first time.

"Sure," I say.

"Dinner too?" he asks.

"That would be great," I say. "I'm hungry."

"I need to take care of something first," he says.

"What?" I ask.

He pulls me in close and kisses me. His heart beating next to my chest is all that exists now. An entire universe I never want to let go of.

JEFF JUST DROPPED me off at my apartment building. We made plans to go out again tomorrow after work. In the past, I probably would've worried that it was too much too soon. But after what I've lived through the last few weeks, I don't want to waste any time.

Life is fleeting. There are no guarantees. All I want is to grab at it.

I open my apartment door. My roommates are on the couch. "Jennifer should've won," Stefanie calls out.

"Hard agree," Vince says.

"Hot guy summer," I say, repeating what Nolan told me. "All the tweens and Gen X moms must've voted for him."

Stefanie turns to me. "You're all smiles," she says.

"Jeff just dropped me off," I say. "We got dinner."

"Ahh," she says.

"You have mail," Vince says. "I put it on your desk."

I go to my bedroom and see an envelope from Fanny Mae. Probably a closeout statement for my loan. I open it. My name, contact information, and student loan number are at the top of the paper, with a typewritten note below:

We're pleased to let you know this loan has been paid in full. The enclosed check is for the overpayment refund.

The bottom flap of the letter drops down. There's a check attached for *one million dollars*. I stare at it in disbelief and count the zeroes at least ten times to make sure I read it correctly.

I did.

She overpaid it—by a million dollars—a life-changing amount of money.

I can save and invest it so I'll never have to worry about living out of my car again if work becomes scarce again.

Or I can use some of it to make my film…

Posted by Miz_Beleaf

Your Happy Ending

Part Eleven:

The flight from Barcelona to Mallorca is 52 minutes long. I'm sitting with Juliet on my lap, waiting for the plane to take off.

We're starting over in sunny Spain—away from the press, the rumors, and the paparazzi.

I contacted my attorney after finding Kevin's fake Aunt's house empty. I told him I didn't care if he reported our communication to the police because Juliet was missing, and I needed them to find her. I later learned that the fake Aunt was someone Kevin and his mistress doctor had hired from the Gamblers Anonymous meeting where they had met.

After my attorney and I hung up, Dad's house alarm went off. I was worried someone was onto me and fled to a nearby beach. It was night, and I waited alone on the sand in the dark for an update.

Soon after, my attorney called, saying that Kevin's mistress's Mom, aka Dr. Clara Griffin's Mom, Norma Griffin, was about to be arrested for murdering Kevin. The police also had gotten an anonymous tip that Juliet was at her house.

I looked up her address and went there. The police were already at her house. I'll never forget when Liz, *The Underdog* chaperone, walked out with Juliet and handed her to me. I was weeping and shaking so hard I worried I might drop my baby girl.

I'll forever be grateful to Liz, who locked Juliet and herself in a closet and protected her. She had endured the public's wrath, who had wrongly accused her of helping me run away. I apologized for putting her in the situation and thanked her.

The plane starts to roll down the runway, slowly at first, before picking up speed and lifting in the air. We climb thousands of feet, and Juliet starts to cry. The air pressure must be straining her tiny ears. I hold her close to me and kiss her forehead to comfort her.

We're seated next to a window that looks out to a sunny blue sky dotted with a few marshmallow clouds. I face Juliet toward it so she can see the beauty of this world, and she smiles for the first time!

God is good.

There's nowhere else on planet Earth I'd rather be than here with her right now.

Steffed_up
literal tears.

Calming4ce_
This hits hard. Are you going to reach out to my coworker's literary agent?

Miz_Beleaf
I'm moving to Spain to lay low for real. A book would draw too much attention.

Calming4ce_
So it was you?

Miz_Beleaf
...

Justin-Case97

thx for sharing your story with us

Steffed_up

thanks for the happy ending.

Miz_Beleaf

Grateful I got mine.

SIXTY-FIVE

NORMA

One Year Later
July 2022

Norma was thriving and enjoying her newfound fame at the all-women's correctional facility in West Virginia.

Even if her daughter had never appreciated her, Norma had amassed countless fans in and out of prison who wanted to hear from her by mail and in person.

They lined up each week to meet with her during the correctional facility's visiting hours and brought her gifts—drawings and paintings of Oreo and her, hand-sewn prairie dresses, and stuffed animal monkeys.

She, in turn, regaled them with her life story about a woman with infinite promise who had fought against a society determined to box her in. To strangle her. To never allow her to become the person she had always been destined to be, so much so that she had to go to prison to finally be seen.

Penguin Random House eventually approached her

about a book deal for her memoir, and she secured a literary agent. She learned there was a precedent for writing and releasing a book in prison. She could even earn royalties there.

Each morning, Norma woke up and wrote one thousand words. She had a contract to fulfill and deadlines to meet. Most importantly, the world couldn't wait to get their hands on her book.

One day, while busy writing in her cell, a wiry guard approached her.

"Working on your big comeback?" he asked.

"I *hate* that word," Norma scolded him.

"What's wrong with a comeback?" he said. "Everyone loves a good comeback story."

"I never went anywhere," Norma responded. "The world finally woke up."

"Gotcha," he said. "Some news about your daughter, huh?"

"What news?" Norma asked him.

"She was found guilty of attempted murder of Jennifer Addis and sentenced to prison," he said.

Norma took it in. She thought about how Cookie would fare on the inside and knew her daughter wouldn't do well. No one there would care that Cookie had ever been a doctor, which would vex her.

A couple of weeks later, when Cookie arrived at Norma's all-women's correctional facility, Norma decided to greet her daughter cordially.

"It's nice to see you, Cookie," Norma said.

"My name is Dr. Clara Griffin," Cookie shot back.

Norma nodded her head and smiled, placating her.

She had never felt proud to say she had a daughter who

was a doctor because Cookie had stolen that dream from Norma.

But now, in prison, Cookie was a nobody—a cipher—a zero.

And Norma was a legend.

How it always should have been.

SIXTY-SIX

LIZ

FOR IMMEDIATE RELEASE

Los Angeles, California — July 25, 2022 — Triple S Production Company is excited to announce its upcoming film *Moving On*, a poignant exploration of second-chance love, loss, and self-discovery.

The film follows Elle, played by newcomer Ruby Coast, a woman navigating the emotional turmoil of a breakup as she hires a kind-hearted mover, Stefan, played by Nolan Jett, winner of the first season of *The Underdog,* to help transition her from a luxury apartment shared with her ex to her new life. Stefan, an artist struggling to make ends meet, shares his own story of heartbreak, revealing the artwork painted on his van.

When Elle unpacks her boxes, she is thrust into an alternate reality filled with the lavish life she could have had with her ex, only to discover her profound loneliness beneath the surface. The film takes a dramatic turn when a missing box leads her to reconnect with Stefan, resulting in another unexpected journey into an alternate reality—where love flourishes between the two leads, yet tragedy looms.

After a heart-wrenching turn of events, including the tragic loss of Stefan, the film culminates in a viral moment that brings Elle's late lover's art to the forefront, igniting a posthumous success that challenges her ideas about legacy, love, and the fleeting nature of life.

Moving On will mark Elizabeth Blau's feature directing debut. She is represented by attorney Jeffrey Abrams. Principal photography is set to begin today in Los Angeles.

For press inquiries, please contact Abrams LLP.

"Is this real life?" I ask Jeff while holding the physical copy of *Variety* he brought me.

"It is," he says.

He came to set today to cheer me on since it's the first day of filming.

"Thank you for being here," I say.

"Wouldn't have missed it for the world," he says, taking my hand and touching the engagement ring on my finger—a single solitaire diamond on a white gold band. It was his Mom's. My soon-to-be mother-in-law told me she wanted me to have it because of her wonderful marriage with Jeff's Dad. I feel honored to wear it and am excited to get married again. We moved in together, and our wedding is in six months.

This will be my second marriage, and while I never felt my ex was my soulmate, I feel Jeff is. Sometimes, I wonder if God brought us together. Jeff's family Rabbi is going to be our officiant. Since this will be Jeff's first marriage, he wants to pull out all the stops—to break the glass under the chuppah, for guests to lift us on chairs while singing Hava Nagila. A month ago, we commissioned an artist to hand-paint a personalized Ketubah.

After my near-death experience in Norma Griffin's basement, I started going to temple again with Jeff for Friday night Shabbat services. For too long, I had been scared that doing so would bring up memories with my Mom, which would cause me pain because of how much I miss her. But I feel differently now. My memories with her are gifts I want to hold onto and not run away from.

"I checked your Dad's flight," Jeff says. "It's scheduled to arrive on time. I'll pick him up this afternoon and bring him here."

"Thanks," I say.

"You have people waiting for you," Jeff says, pointing to Stefanie, Vince, Erika, and Svetlana, who all came for a show of support. I hug him and walk over to them.

"I'm proud of you," Stefanie says, hugging me.

"I can't wait to see your film on the big screen," Vince says.

"Thanks for being such good friends," I say.

Erika turns to me, "I knew this day would come."

"Thank you for always believing in me," I say.

"I'm still waiting for my role," Svetlana says.

"Next time," I say.

"Promise?" she asks.

I love her—always with an eye on the prize.

I invited two people today who aren't here—Ava, who's on vacation with her new boyfriend. I'm happy she's giving love a second chance after her late husband's death. I'm also glad she got justice for his murder. After Clara Griffin was implicated in Juliet's kidnapping, the police seized her phone and found texts between her and Kevin Addis, orchestrating Neil Katz's office fire and planning Jennifer's death. Ava was right—Neil never started the fire that killed him with a cigarette. Now, Clara faces additional charges for Neil's murder on top of the charges for Jennifer's attempted murder, which she was found guilty of.

Speaking of Jennifer, she's the other person I invited who isn't here today. After her final performance on *The Underdog*, she told me she was moving to Spain. She wanted to give Juliet the gift of a normal childhood and didn't think she could do it here with the unending press attention. She said the trip to Los Angeles was too far to make to be here today. I hope she's found the peace she deserves. I'll forever be grateful for her generosity. Without her, I wouldn't be here today, realizing my dream.

"I better get to work," I tell my friends. They nod and clap as I walk to my director's chair.

It took a decade, and I could've never imagined the path that would lead me here. But I'm finally on set about to direct my first feature film. After everything I've been through, from living in my car to what I went through while working at *The Underdog*, I'm that much more thankful for this chance.

I sit in my chair with DIRECTOR printed on its cloth back.

This is really happening.

I look at the camera monitor as the actors take their marks and see *her*. She made it. It's Jennifer, and she's holding Juliet's hand, who's now old enough to walk. I look up from the camera and smile at them both.

"Break a leg," she says, smiling back at me.

"Thank you," I say.

I take a deep breath in. It's go-time.

"Ready, quiet on set, please," I say.

Everything goes still.

"Roll camera," I say.

"Camera rolling," the camera operator says.

"Roll sound," I say.

"Sound rolling," the sound mixer says.

The second assistant camerawoman moves in with the clapperboard.

"Moving on. Scene one. Slate one. Take one," she says, snapping the clapperboard shut.

"Action," I say.

At last.

FIFTEEN YEARS LATER

NORMA GRIFFIN, DOC# 1569837
WOMEN'S CORRECTIONAL FACILITY
12374 STATION WAY
ALDERSON, WV 24910

Dear Norma,

Since my Mom was released from prison, we've had a lot of catching up to do.

I already knew that you tried to break up my parents, switched me at birth with a dead baby, and killed my Dad from all the articles written about you and your "memoir."

But Mom shared something new. She said you hated the name she gave me because I wasn't named after you. Bet you're happy the Romanos scrapped Rose.

Honestly, I'm happy about it too. Rose doesn't fit me at all. Do you know what the kids at my high school call me? Take a guess…

Sadie the Sadist.

Anyone who knows me knows why. Mom says you'll be released in a few weeks. Guess you'll find out why soon too.

Hope you enjoy your last days in the clink. I've heard re-entry can be hard.

I'll be waiting for you.

Sadie

THE END

(or just the beginning...)

ACKNOWLEDGMENTS

I want to thank you. Yes, YOU, for reading. In this life, few things are as precious as one's time, and you chose to spend some of your time reading my words.

I wrote this book to be a fun, popcorn thriller. To hopefully transport you away from the struggles of daily life and give you an escape. If I succeeded, I'm so glad. If I didn't, I still want to thank you for being here and reading.

One of the best parts about writing books is connecting with readers. If you'd like to reach out, I do my best to respond to all messages:

Email: contactsagit@gmail.com
Instagram/Threads: @sagitschwartz
TikTok: sagitwriter

www.ingramcontent.com/pod-product-compliance
Lightning Source LLC
Chambersburg PA
CBHW071533110726
47908CB00007B/1874